William Howe Downes

Spanish Ways and By-Ways

with a glimpse of the Pyrenees

William Howe Downes

Spanish Ways and By-Ways
with a glimpse of the Pyrenees

ISBN/EAN: 9783337406011

Printed in Europe, USA, Canada, Australia, Japan

Cover: Foto ©Andreas Hilbeck / pixelio.de

More available books at **www.hansebooks.com**

SPANISH WAYS AND BY-WAYS

WITH

A GLIMPSE OF THE PYRENEES

BY

WILLIAM HOWE DOWNES

ILLUSTRATED

BOSTON
CUPPLES, UPHAM & COMPANY
Old Corner Bookstore
1883

PRESS OF
STANLEY AND USHER,
BOSTON.

CONTENTS.

LIST OF ILLUSTRATIONS.

CHAPTER I.

I LOVE the South. The people there are lazy, — true; they are shiftless, — yes; they are immoral, — let us admit it; there is dirt and decay in the place of cleanliness and growth, stagnation where there should be progress! Well, in spite of all these dreadful things, I love the southern lands. Why? I hardly know. Perhaps I have a sneaking sympathy for laziness, and immorality, and dirt, and decay. Some of us need to learn how to be idle gracefully. The Andalusians will, I am sure, teach such a lesson in a most unconscious way to any wayfarer who happens along.

The Salon was about to close; Paris was becoming dull, comparatively speaking; it happens to the best of Americans to get tired of Paris sometimes. We had "done" the town quite thoroughly. (I have heard of a tourist who said, "*We done Rome*, when we was there before.") What had we seen? Well, Prudhon, as *Bellac*, in " Le Monde où l'on s'ennuie," with his "au delà" and his delicious theory of Platonic

love ; and Samary* the Pretty, as *Suzanne ;* Krauss, as
Hermosa, in the " Tribut de Zamora," which, begging
M. Gounod's pardon, will never stir the roots of the
spectator's hair as much as one simple little melody in
" Faust."   Then there was the " Huguenots," mounted
as I have never seen an opera mounted before or
since ; I remember particularly the scene of the second
act, representing the castle and gardens of Chenon-
ceaux, with an immense perspective, where a river
winds away through the distant landscape which lies
there under a flood of daylight and stretches leagues
away : —

> " O beau pays de la Touraine,
>   Riants jardins, verte fontaine,
>   Ruisseau qui murmures à peine,
>   Que sur tes bords j'aime à rêver."

We had also seen the " Hamlet " of M. Thomas,
with a ballet.   Fancy the operatic Hamlet (it was
M. Faure) singing his soliloquy at the audience, and
then contemplating with rapture a splendid ballet.

Better than all these diversions, — better than the
tiresome Salon, with its sensational and clap-trap
torture-chamber scenes, its studio-model goddesses of
pagandom, its acres of idealess canvases ten feet
by fourteen, — memory recalls with ever-increasing
pleasure certain rainy afternoons passed in the Louvre.
Furthermore, we had breakfasted at that incompar-
able restaurant on the terrace of Saint Germain ; we

---

* She will never again be photographed while smiling: for in this country they have utilized
her portrait in an advertisement of somebody's tooth-powder.

had strolled about over the airy hill of Saint Cloud ; we had passed at least three delightful evenings at the Besselièvre open-air concerts.

And one balmy evening, as we sat smoking our Manilas, on a certain quaint stone balcony looking down into a great paved court, Hermano said : —

" Let's go to Spain ! "

It was not the first time that the subject had been broached. We had been devouring books about Spain for a month ; but each time that the project was discussed it was gravely decided not to go to Spain. The folly of going there in midsummer was pointed out to us ; we realized the objections, but the idea would not be dismissed. It was a case of " now or never," or we chose so to consider it. There are so few untrodden paths now left in Europe, that Spain, which looks compact and accessible on the map, offers no small temptation to the traveler who unreasonably desires to get out of the beaten track. One supposes that more or less French and English is spoken everywhere nowadays — but don't suppose so, reader. Except in Madrid, the traveler may have his choice between Spanish or the language of deaf-mutes. Do not go to Spain unless you know the lingo. It is a very beautiful language, but no language sounds well to him who does not understand it. The dearth of French-speaking and English-speaking natives would not be so awkward a circumstance if a good guide-book existed. The Joanne handbooks published by

Hachette of Paris, and Murray's "Spain," edited by
Ford, are faulty and untrustworthy in many particu-
lars. Baedecker, the best guidebook-maker in the
world, has not included Spain in his series, a fact
which is often lamented by travelers in that country,
and with good cause. The lack of a good guidebook
becomes a real misfortune in a land almost destitute

of good hôtels, and until within a very few years without any of the most ordinary "modern improvements."

It is no easy undertaking to lay out a route through
Spain which takes in all the interesting points, without
involving more or less doubling on your own tracks.
Granada, for instance, is a *cul-de-sac*, and there is but
one way of getting into or out of it by rail. In the
absence of a trustworthy guidebook, the following
itinerary may be found interesting if not useful to

those contemplating a short trip on the Peninsula ·
Bayonne, Vittoria, Burgos, Valladolid, Madrid, Toledo,
Cordova, Seville, Cadiz, Gibraltar, Malaga, **Granada,**
Alicante, Valencia, Barcelona, Perpignan. **This is**
substantially the route we laid out before leaving Paris,
but the heat was so overpowering, that it was **materi-**
ally abridged, and the surplus time thereby **gained
was devoted to a** run through **the Lower** Pyrenees.
This route is all rail as far as Cadiz, and involves several days of steamboat travel **on the Mediterranean**
between Malaga and Barcelona. **It would be found**
long enough and **comprehensive enough by** most
travelers. To be **sure, it** leaves out Saragossa, Sego-
via, Ronda, and Cartagena. When **the** new **route**
from France under **the Pyrenees shall have been**
completed, **an** entirely **new** plan **of** campaign will **be**
made possible, and the Spanish tour, **now becoming so**
popular among the **French,** may be accomplished with
greater **ease and** economy. At present it is idle to
deny that a " pleasure " journey **as such is rather a**
grim sort of enterprise **for any but the most enthusias-**
tic and dauntless of **travelers. The day will** come,
though, when it will **be as common for the** Cooky to
go whirling through the passes of the Pyrenees *en
route* for Lisbon and Tangiers, **as** it is now for the
same ubiquitous individual to sail up the Rhine on his
way into Switzerland ; and the time **is not** far distant
when **the** great American tourist will multitudinously
swarm through **the** gardens of **the Alcazar** and cut his

initials on the walls of the Alhambra. It has been a true saying that the Pyrenees separated Europe from Africa, but, in the nature of things, that cannot last forever. Even Spain is beginning to feel the influence of the nineteenth-century spirit. Soon enough her shiftless picturesqueness, her squalid grandeur, and her lazy dignity, will give way before the dead commonplace of practical modern industry and thrift.

A word as to this modest narrative. Some parts of it appeared in two Boston newspapers. In its present form it has been revised throughout, and augmented. Certain entertaining and harmless exaggerations which enlivened the original text have been modified or expunged : not because I am narrow enough to confine myself to facts unnecessarily, but because on reading Théophile Gautier, Alexandre Dumas, and Edmondo de Amicis, I perceive not only that there is no need for me to tamper with the truth, but that, in point of fact, the best way for me to get a reputation for originality is to be truthful. Gautier's book is thoroughly delightful. A genius has a right to lie ; but *nous autres* — never ! Furthermore, I would ask the reader to look upon the record of this journey as the most off-hand of vacation sketches, in which I have aimed to avoid flippancy on the one hand and pedantry on the other. If the reader has a mania for the Picturesque, and a not over-fastidious stomach, let him then mentally pack his kit and be ready for a start.

CHAPTER II.

THE direct route from Paris to Spain is by the Orléans railroad, via Orléans, Tours, Angoulême, Bordeaux, and Bayonne. Sleeping-cars are run through from Paris to Madrid over this line. Berths are an expensive luxury in Europe, however, — about five dollars extra for a night, and it may be fancied that they are not largely patronized. The Europeans generally do not take kindly to American railroad improvements.

There was a sunset when we rode down to the Orléans station in Paris — a sunset more splendid than any German chromo-lithograph, full of crimson-lake and chrome-yellow as a conflagration. We had just dined, and being unaware that we were not to eat a first-rate dinner for at least a month to come, were in high spirits and full of pleasant anticipations. The smooth rolling of the wheels of our victoria over the asphalt was as music in our ears. We passed the garden of the Tuileries and the Louvre (do you remember how D'Artagnan got Anne of Austria, and the young king, and Mazarin, away from the rebellious city?) ; crossed to the monumental Island of the Cité and whirled rapidly around to the rear of Our Lady of Paris (how

fine those flying buttresses are!) ; peeped shudder-
ingly into the open door of the horrible Morgue as we
passed ; and when, on the other side of the Seine, we
rattled along abreast of the shadowy Jardin des
Plantes, looked back to see the river with its noble
bridges, the great cathedral towers, and the whole
stirring panorama of the town bathed in a liquid,
changeful glory of color, so superb that it might well
have been taken for a good omen.

The night train for the South left at half-past eight,
and for three hours we sat chatting by the window of
our carriage while we were rattled swiftly through the
long, sleeping stretches of moonlit country ; and our
talk was of the land of the Cid, of Cervantes, of Murillo, of Velasquez, of Moorish palaces and mosques,
of bull-fights, of cathedrals, of "castles in Spain."
All this, from a subject of conversation, shortly became
a subject for dreams ; and it must be confessed that
we were surprised when we opened our eyes to find
ourselves in Bordeaux at about seven in the morning.
Bordeaux! What a strangely familiar sound the
name had, yet we had never been there before. We
jumped out of the carriage and had some very bad
coffee and rolls by way of breakfast, then bought some
novels, and settled ourselves down for a tedious ride
through Gascony. A dreary desert of sand, Les
Landes, was crossed, and about noon the train arrived
at Bayonne, the last town of consequence in France.
A little river, the Bidassoa, divides France from Spain,

and after crossing it the first station is Irun, where the
Spanish customs-officers were awaiting us. The examination of baggage is not much more than a empty
form; nothing but the largest trunks are opened, and
the operation is soon over. It is necessary to change
cars here, for the Spanish railways are of a wider

gauge than the French. The frontier is no sooner
crossed than one notices the different characteristics
of people, buildings, carriages, ways, and surroundings,
in a score of respects. A long delay occurs — more
than half an hour after the train and passengers are
ready. Finally a workman comes along and deliber-
ately splices a new tassel on to the cord of the window-
shade in our compartment. "Ah!" sighs an old
Frenchman sitting near us, "one sees well that one is
in Spain. Ordinarily that is done in the workshops."
On this we lead him into conversation. He has lived
in Spain half the time for the past ten or twelve years,
having established a manufactory somewhere near
Saragossa. He says Spain is just one century behind
the times, and he goes on to draw a gloomy picture of
her condition — "devoured by the church and the army."
On the railways no attention whatever is paid to the

comfort of the passengers; the eating is not fit for
human beings; honesty is utterly unknown; there is
no security for property; everyone lives in sloth and
squalor and ignorance; and more of the same tenor.
He told several amusing anecdotes.   In winter, he
said, they have foot-warmers filled with hot water to
place in the railway carriages.   At a station a passenger opens the door and calls out to the guard that the
foot-warmer is cold.   The guard goes and orders a
third party to replace the cold foot-warmer by a warm
one.   It is apparently done, and the various functionaries receive their "gratification" (fee), but after
leaving the station the passenger discovers that the
new foot-warmer is as cold as a stone.   The lazy
rascals had shifted the foot-warmers about from one
carriage to another.   A second anecdote was to this
effect.   A poor widow was moving her domicile from
one town to another, and had sent a boxful of clothing
and bedding by express to her prospective home.
When the box was opened there was nothing in it
but stones and gravel.   The widow complained in due
form to the forwarding company, whose representatives shrugged their shoulders and said it was "too
bad."   *Voilà tout !*   While the Gaul was regaling us
with these and similar histories, we were moving at
a very sedate pace through " the Normandy of Spain,"
a remarkably picturesque, but not a remarkably fertile,
region, except by comparison with other parts of the
Peninsula.   At San Sebastian, a finely situated coast

town, now a favorite summer resort, a party of six or
seven men besieged our compartment, and handed in
one valise after another, together with hat-boxes,
baskets, parcels, and rugs enough for a large family;
each one talking very volubly all the time. We supposed they were all going to Madrid, at least, but it
turned out that only one of them was going at all,
that all the traps belonged to him, and that the others
had come to see him off. Consequently, when the
dinner-bell and the fire alarm-bell and the gong and
the whistle had all sounded for the purpose of announ-
cing that the train would start in five or ten minutes,
the traveler was embraced by each
of his friends and received at least
a dozen parting speeches. Then he
settled back in his seat, tipped his
hat to us, and lighted a cigarette with
an air of sad determination. He
traveled as much as thirty miles, and
then left us. I think he had made
his will before starting, and looked
upon himself as a great traveler.

The railway soon quits the coast
of the Bay of Biscay and enters
among the highly romantic Canta-
brian Mountains, where the train
plunges noisily through a seemingly
interminable succession of tunnels. It was among
these rock-bound defiles that the Carlists carried on

their prolonged guerilla war against the government,
inflicting an untold amount of damage upon the
region, which still shows traces of their wanton de-
structiveness.   No country could be better adapted
to the desultory warfare waged by these bandits.   The
whole region, a succession of gaunt, rocky ridges and
deep ravines, peaks with the fantastic resemblance of
architectural forms so frequently observed in these
mountain chains, mysterious caverns and forests, gorges
and cascades, — all suggested the *contrabandista*, the
robber, and the kindred heroes celebrated in all literature relating to Spain.   " Mountain fastnesses " became
an intelligible phrase to me, and at each bend in the
road I half expected to see, peering over a rocky
breastwork, the stern visage and fantastic headgear of
a Carlist sentinel, with leveled rifle, demanding the
watchword.   However, nothing half so romantic as
that occurred.   We presently stopped at the station
of Miranda for dinner ; it was half-past eight in the
evening, for on Spanish railways and indeed in Spain
generally there is no such thing as a regular hour for
meals.   Having heard so much said about the miserable quality of Spanish cookery, we were pleasantly
disappointed in the repast at Miranda, which was not
intolerably bad by any means.   As we learned later,
Miranda is one of the three or four places where you
can get a good meal.   After leaving this oasis in the
dreary desert of bad food into which we had plunged,
we entered the province of Old Castile, and at half-
past ten arrived at the ancient capital — Burgos.

CHAPTER III.

BURGOS is doubtless the most interesting town in
the north of Spain; but it is the little things that impress one in traveling, and our first plunge was not
encouraging. None of the hôtels are unreservedly
recommended. As a choice of evils we had deter-
mined to try the Fonda del Norte. At first it seemed
as if we were not destined to find any lodging at all.
The omnibus bearing the name of the hôtel stood at
the door of the station, and entering it promptly, we
handed the little numbered slip of paper, called a "bul-
letin" (the nearest approach the effete nations have
made to a baggage-check), to the driver, who disap-
peared in the direction of the baggage-room. A
charming half-hour passed away before he returned
with the trunk. In the meantime I had got out of the
omnibus twice, and had looked in at the baggage-
room to see how affairs were progressing. The driver
and eight porters were engaged in an animated conversation. No one present spoke French, so I
conceived the happy idea of talking very loud to the
driver in English, repeating the word "*equipages*"
(baggage) at frequent intervals, and occasionally
putting my hand into my pocket, as if I were about

to haul forth a small fortune.   In a few moments the
trunk was forthcoming.   We were conveyed some
distance, through narrow, winding streets, under arch-
ways dimly lighted, and past great, dark buildings with
grated windows, until at last the infernal racket made
by a rapidly driven omnibus in roughly paved streets
ceased abruptly, the door of the vehicle was thrown
open, and we were about to descend when a frowzy
woman, speaking what she thought was French,
appeared and informed us that the inn was full, owing
to to-morrow's fête, namely, the festival of Saints Peter
and Paul, which was to be brilliantly celebrated, etc.
After she had been talking fifteen or twenty minutes,
we begged her to come to the point and tell us the
worst at once.   Thus it happened that at midnight
we were taken to a private house where there was a
room which we might occupy until the pressure of
business at the Fonda del Norte should be over.   The
driver knocked thunderously at the *porte-cochère* of
a tall, stuccoed building, and it opened, admitting our
forlorn group.   We were conducted up a picturesque
stone staircase, through such a stiff odor of the stable
that I fancied there was some mistake, and that we
had been brought to the wrong building, but such
was not the case.   Incredible as it may appear, the
very worthy and respectable people who received us
as lodgers live in the midst of that stifling odor, which
fills every room in the vast house, and, I am forced to
conclude that they, and the natives generally, like it.

Our hosts could not easily get used to the notion
that we did not speak Spanish, and, consequently,
they plied us with questions and seemed to regard our
replies — a rather ingenious mixture of French, Latin,

and deaf-and-dumb language — as very comical, as
they doubtless were. All in all, it was a great lark
for the elderly lady and her two pretty daughters, and
it was not without a good deal of laughter that we
made them understand that we were Americans, that
the hôtel was full, that we had been sent to them for
a night's lodging, that we should tearfully take our
leave in the morning, and that we needed no food or
drink before retiring. It was on this occasion that

the hollow pretensions of a Spanish phrasebook
bought in Paris were shown up. It had nothing in it
but such remarks as " Will this telegram go to-day?"
(!) "This pair of boots does not fit me," "Steward,
bring me a basin," etc., which, it may be conceived,
did not help us much. However, though the book
was worthless, it contained no such suggestive
or alarming dialogues as the following, which M.
Théophile Gautier found in his Spanish phrasebook,
under the caption, "Arrival at the Inn": *Traveler* —
" I would like to take something, as I am very hungry." *Landlord* — "Take a chair!" *Traveler* — "But
I would like to take something to eat!" *Landlord* —
" Well, what have you brought with you?" The
traveler sadly admits that he has brought no victuals
with him, so then the landlord shows him the butch-
er's shop and the bakery, and adds: " If you will go
and get some meat and bread, I think my wife will
probably cook the things for you." Whereupon the
traveler grows furious and abusive, after which he
quiets down and does as he is bid, but on his departure he pays, among other items in his bill, " Row, 8
reales."

The town was very noisy that night, and many
musically disposed persons seemed to be abroad, cel-
ebrating in advance the festival of the two saints.
The room where we found ourselves was as full of
subtle odors as the air was full of startling sounds.
The door refused to be locked and the windows would

not be shut. We looked for a trap in the floor, but found none, and concluded that the audible conversation in the adjoining room did not concern the manner of our taking off or the subsequent disposition of our mortal remains ; and so presently we succumbed to the drowsy god, and were as much at home as any wanderers may be who sleep and forget where they are

We found our way back to the Fonda del Norte early in the morning, and the linguist, looking more frowzy than ever, talked us upstairs and into the best rooms in the house. The hôtel smelled as badly as the house where we had slept, but differently, — it was a more elaborate odor. Still, it was not so powerful and rank as the scent which the streets could furnish, and after opening the windows for awhile, it was decided to shut them. Soon Hermano went out, holding his handkerchief to his nose, and shortly came back in triumph with a bottle of Cologne-water !

"If you think you have smelled Burgos yet," he gasped, "you are mistaken. You have not been to the Plaza Mayor. I never until now appreciated the force of Marcellus's remark, 'Something is rotten in the state of Denmark.' The greatest man Europe has produced — since the Cid — is John Mary Farina."

An uninviting breakfast of hard white bread and coffee with queer milk was served in the long, narrow, and dark dining-room, where unhappily the windows were open. Then we found a small boy who spoke a few words of French, and we set forth for the cathedral, hugging the shady sides of the streets, for it was growing very warm.   The exterior of the cathedral must have been wonderfully effective before it was defaced by the "alterations" of some vandal architect, who evidently considered the pure Gothic a very bad style, and tried to improve the front by converting it into a Romanesque monstrosity.   The spires, of wonderfully elaborate and airy open-work in stone, are happily left intact as originally constructed.   There is no good view of the building to be had, as it is surrounded by mean structures, but there are a good many "bits" of detail which are very beautiful.   We were glad enough to get into the cool interior, where an occasional whiff of incense (not ordinarily a grateful perfume to heterodox nostrils) was very welcome. The chief charm of all the great Spanish churches lies in the wonderful wealth of interior decoration and detail, upon which art and industry have lavished all their best endeavors for centuries ; and to this there is but one exception to be made, namely, the Seville cathedral, which, while it excels all others in its artistic and material treasures, is yet remarkable principally by virtue of its superb proportions and majestic size. The Burgos cathedral is a great museum and treasure-house, containing countless chapels filled by rich altars, princely tombs, elaborate *retablos*, and precious works of art.   Not far from the entrance a young priest, lantern-jawed and hungry-looking, took us in

charge, and sadly showed us the wonders of the place,
accepting a couple of timidly proferred *pesetas* at the
close of the exercises. He spoke French — the sort
of French that Spaniards speak. It is not like the
French of Stratford-atte-Bowe, yet, much to the profit
and pleasure of all concerned, we understood each
other. I wish I could remember the conversation,
for it must have been somewhat amusing on both
sides. Something in the young man's manner made
me feel sympathy for him; he seemed out of place
amid his surroundings; he wanted to know so many
things about the great world outside; and he seemed
a very human and modern pattern of a Spanish priest
to spend his days in such a place. Yet how fine, how
grand it is, this monument of a faith which has done
more than move mountains! It is no part of my
intention to describe it. But there are two sensational
objects of curiosity which ought not to be passed by.
The first is the Cid's coffer. This enormous iron-bound
chest, as capacious as the most inordinate Saratoga
trunk, is to be seen in the chapter-house, where it is
falling to pieces from age. The story runs that the
Cid was "short" just before he started for one of his
campaigns in the South; and in order to raise the
necessary funds, he filled this and another similar
chest with sand, then presenting them to two Hebrews
as collateral security for an enormous loan, represented the contents to be gold and silver ware; thus
he obtained the required cash, so well was he known

to the money-lenders as an honorable knight. On
his return he faithfully repaid the loan with a good
round interest : —

> " Y á los honrados Judios
> Raquel y Vidas llevad
> Docientos marcos de oro,
> Tantos de plata, y no mas,
> Que me endonaron prestados
> Cuando me parti á lidiar
> Sobre dos cofres de arena
> Debajo de mi verdad ;
> Y rogadles de mi parte
> Que me quieran perdonar
> Que con acuita lo fice
> De mi gran necesidad.
> Que aunque cuidan que es arena
> Lo que en los cofres esta,
> Quedó soterrado en ella
> El oro de mi verdad."

The other curiosity is a life-size effigy of Jesus on
the cross, known as " the Christ of Burgos." As a
specimen of the art of wood-carving it is exceedingly
interesting and even wonderful. But it is revolting
in its realistic representation of physical anguish.
The expression of intense suffering in the drawn lines
of the face, the agonized movement of the emaciated
trunk and limbs, the rills of crimson blood which
trickle from the wounds, — everything, — is brutally
set forth in the good old Spanish way, which leaves
nothing to the imagination. Some writers have been
informed, and apparently have believed, that the figure

was a stuffed human skin, but the fiction is as absurd as the legend, which states that it floated miraculously from the Holy Land over the seas to Burgos. The comparatively unknown sculptor of the sixteenth century whose work it is would no doubt feel flattered if he could know of the tales concerning its origin. The carving of the stalls in the choir, which, as in almost all the Spanish churches, is placed in the centre of the nave in just such a position as to destroy the best perspective of the interior, is also a work of great intricacy and beauty. Seldom has wood been wrought into nobler forms than in some of the twenty chapels, where the bones of many a deceased grandee of Castile lie entombed under superb monuments of marble and bronze. The few paintings of value in these chapels, including one by Sebastian del Piombo and one by Ribera, can be seen to very ill advantage in the half-light of the gruesome recesses where they are placed.

We climbed to the highest perch inside the spire, to obtain a panoramic view of the town. The bells rang a noisy noonday peal directly under our feet as we gazed, and the young priest smiled — he was singularly handsome when he smiled — to see us clutch the slight handrail so vigorously, as the airy structure vibrated with the shock of the ringing. We went out by another door, and wandered about the town aimlessly, avoiding the beggars as best we could. One of this tribe, who was seated in a warm corner

in front of a big, massive door, holding out his hand
and muttering mechanical appeals, had a parchment-
like skin of the rich tone of old mahogany, and the
physiognomy of a North American Indian, modified
by some very decided Irish
characteristics. He wore
sandals, but they were a
useless luxury. The coat of
dirt on his feet would have
been sufficient protection.
The beggars in Bur-
gos are numerous but
not aggressive ; it is
only in Granada that
they wage open
warfare upon stran-
gers, pursue them,
surround them,
threaten them,
curse them, and
mob them when an
opportunity offers.
After the cathedral,
Burgos has a few
minor objects of in-
terest to show the
stranger : among these are the house of the Cid, the
Cid's tomb, several chapels containing finely carved
altars and tombs ; and, at a little distance from the city,

the Carthusian convent of Miraflores, famous formerly
as one of the richest monasteries in the country, and
the asylum of only the most blue-blooded nuns, the
daughters of the aristocracy esteeming it a privilege
to be interred alive in such a fine place.

Perhaps there is nothing more interesting in the
place, however, than the Plaza Mayor, where, during
the fête, the people congregated to chat and idle away
the time.

The noonday meal at the Fonda del Norte was one
of the most mysterious repasts we had ever encountered. Not a single dish was in the least degree like
any dish we had ever tasted before, and to this day we
suspect that one of the most alluring courses consisted
of donkey's meat stewed in rancid oil. The salad
looked well, but gave forth the same odor as the soup,
which it would not be proper to characterize as it
merits. We left the table, hungry.

BY THE CATHEDRAL WALL.

CHAPTER IV.

IT will be many years before public opinion demands or permits the abolition of the national amusement. You are told by a certain class of Spaniards, who are inclined to be very sensitive and self-conscious, that bull-fighting as an institution is falling into merited disrepute; that they themselves consider it barbarous and disgusting, and that it will not be long before it will be abolished; in proof of which they point out the efforts constantly making in the Cortes for the legal prohibition of the sport. The people who talk in this way are, I think, perfectly sincere; but they are in a very small minority. New rings have lately been built in many towns, and fine arenas are supported by comparatively small cities. That the opponents of bull-fighting form but a very inconsiderable proportion of even the higher classes in Spain is demonstrated by the practical unanimity with which the aristocracy and the well-to-do folk of the large cities present themselves in their upholstered boxes each Sunday afternoon, in precisely the same way that the belles and swells of London or Paris drop in at the opera on subscription nights; and by the foundation, in 1882, of a new periodical devoted exclusively to the *arte taurino.* The genuine *lidiadores* regard the profession as worthy of the respect due to a branch of the arts. If the bull-fight may not be justified on any ground, it may be immensely dignified, and the self-respect of the spectators very much strengthened, by a judicious employment of the phrase " el arte taurino."

It is only on special holidays that the provincial towns have bull-fights. Madrid, Barcelona, Seville have them regularly each Sunday throughout the spring and summer. A *corrida extraordinaria* is usually more interesting — being a special occasion, which draws out a special crowd — than a *corrida de abono*, which is the usual weekly performance, and is more probably attended by a *blasé* or over-critical audience. For, it is unnecessary to say, the audience is always at least as interesting for the foreigner as the combat.

The tickets, in the large towns, are numbered, like theatre tickets. Here is a Madrid ticket: —

PLAZA DE TOROS.

IIᴬ CORRIDA DE ABONO.

GRADA 10 SOMBRA.	TERCERA FILA, No. 22, DIEZ REALES.

Consérvese este billete durante la corrida.

A rude cut of a bull's head, two banners, and a *torero* ornament the face of the ticket.

In Burgos everybody turned out with the open intention of " making a day of it." The ring accommodates eight thousand people, and the performance begins at five P. M. We bought seats *à la sombra* (in the shade), which are dearer than those *al sol,* of course, the price being three pesetas each. Foreigners find it easier to calculate prices in pesetas than in reales, because a peseta is exactly the same as a French franc, while a real is equivalent to five cents. The tickets are not numbered in Burgos, as they are in Madrid, and it was necessary to go early. So we set forth at three o'clock. To find the way to the *plaza de toros* it was only necessary to follow the crowd. The general absence of sidewalks made no difference now, as the street was filled from one side to the other with the throng. Fan merchants and *aguadores*, or water-pedlars, everywhere drove a thriving trade. It was very hot and dusty, and in Spain the two principal occupations in summer are fanning and drinking water. It seems un-European to drink cold water freely, and in that respect, as in many others, Spain is un-European. Gautier says it is a part of Africa, and should still belong to the Moors by right. The aguadores carry their staple in earthen jugs of beautiful form, and usually receive a cent for a glass of water. Their cry, " Quien quiere agua?" ("Who wants water?") is shrill and plaintive. Before serving a client they invariably pour a few drops of the precious liquid into the glass, rinse the inside of it out with their brown fingers, throw away the water thus used, and refill the glass from one of their jugs. They also carry a sort of white confectionery, the size of a small breakfast-roll, of the

consistency of a piece of honeycomb, which you can dip in the water and suck with great satisfaction; it absorbs the water and melts away gradually in the mouth.

The ring is just outside the town, and you pass at least a score of side-shows and a hundred booths

before you reach it, with your boots powdered by the
dust.   At last you are inside, and have found a seat
in the shade.   It is a fine spectacle, and suggests a
glorified circus.   The array of colors is simply dazzling.
Every woman has a fan, and if she is not holding it
up to screen her face from the overpowering rays of
the sun, she is going through those thousand-and-one
manœuvres with it, of which only a Spanish woman
knows the secret, and after seeing which you find the
fan drill of other women unspeakably awkward and
flat.   The fan is never motionless for the hundredth
part of a second.   While you are saying "Scat!" it is
opened and shut, and fluttered, waved, and flirted
until your head swims, and you are only conscious
of seeing a hazy area of bright color, through which
a pair of soft black eyes may be looking at you and
through you as innocently as possible.   All Spanish
women have the gift of wielding the fan born in them;
it is not acquired.   The tiniest female infant, just
learning to toddle about, manipulates a fan in a way
to put to the blush the adult coquette of any other
nationality.   Almost all the Spanish women still wear
the *toca*, or lace head-dress (few *mantillas* are worn
commonly — they are going out), ordinarily of coarse
black lace, and it is immeasurably prettier and more
becoming than any hat or bonnet that ever was
invented.   They affect black dresses also, so that the
fan is, in nine cases out of ten, set off against a dark
background with decided effect.   Nowhere have I

seen prettier girls or handsomer women than among the spectators at this bull-fight in Burgos. The average of beautiful faces was unquestionably fifty per cent. above that of any equally representative crowd in any other European country. Not one blonde, not even a *rousse* or a brown-haired maiden in all the throng. All were uncompromising bru-nettes, with jet black hair, black eyes, and dark complexions. The seats were mere benches, placed so close together that, once in your place, you could not move an inch. The crowd grew larger and more dense at every mo-

ment. Imagine the animation of a House of Representatives on a field-day, of a National Convention, of the meetings of the Massachusetts Temperance Alliance, and quadruple it; then you may have a feeble idea of the commotion, the uproar, and the movement of the audience while waiting for the *corrida* to begin. An incident of the slightest importance was seized upon as a pretext for a riot. A man lost his hat; it was knocked out of the hands of the person who picked it up to return it to the

owner ; it was tossed here and there, and finally fell
into the ring ; instantly there went up a roar from
eight thousand throats such as that which Milton says

> "'Tore hell's concave, and beyond
> Frighted the reign of Chaos and old Night."

So the audience amused themselves while waiting,
and presently family parties here and there produced
huge hampers from which the necks of bottles
protruded, and, opening them, began to eat and drink
as well as be merry. We declined offers of fruit,
wine, cheese, etc., freely made by our generous
neighbors. Mr. Ford says (in Murray's handbook),
that it is the invariable custom to offer to share with
your neighbors in the railway-carriage, or elsewhere,
whatever you are about to eat, drink, or smoke ; but
that such offers are usually declined, or at any rate the
first time. I had noted this, so I began by declining
with thanks, but found I was seldom or never asked
a second time ; whereas, when I passed my cigar-case
about, the proud Castilians present usually omitted to
go through the ceremony of declining the first offer.
Since this is a fair sample of Mr. Ford's information,
or rather misinformation, I need not mention the
other instances of it. His advice with regard to one
point is, however, so rich that is worth while to quote
it : "You will often be asked if you are a Christian,
meaning a Roman Catholic ; your best answer is,
'Christiano, si ; Apostolico Romano, no.'" He takes

it for granted that all his readers are members of the Church of England. Elsewhere he alludes to the Spaniards as "the weaker brethren," in a tone of patronage which is most offensive,* whereas he evidently thinks he is displaying a spirit of great liberality and politeness.

But to return to our bulls. At the appointed hour the *alguacil*, or governor, entered his box and was received with a tremendous storm of cheers, as his coming is always the signal for the beginning. Two cavaliers dressed in black entered the ring on prancing horses, and gravely saluted this authority, who flung the key of the bull-pen to one of them, who attempted to catch it in his hat, but failed and had to dismount to pick it up. This incident produced howls of derision and thunders of laughter.

As soon as the representatives of the civil authority had withdrawn, the band struck up a wild and fantastic march, and the various bull-fighters defiled into the ring and made the circuit of it, saluting the governor in passing before his box. A flutter of excitement passed through the audience. The valiant warriors were arrayed in the most gorgeous costumes imaginable, no two alike, and as the brilliant procession passed slowly along I could think of nothing but Del Puente singing the stirring " Toreador " song in " Carmen."

---

* " Few Spaniards, when traversing a cathedral, pass the high altar without crossing themselves, since the incarnate Host is placed thereon ; and in order not to offend the weaker brethren, every considerate Protestant should also manifest an outward respect for this Holy of Holies of the natives."

The generic name for bull-fighters is *toreros*, but there are various classes, — the *chulos*, the *picadores*, the *banderilleros*, and the *espadas*. The espada is the great hero of the combat, and the vainglorious baritone in Bizet's opera is doubtless meant to be an espada, or, as the star performer in the arena is sometimes called, a *matador*. He is the swordsman who inflicts the fatal thrust upon the fierce victim of the sport. He wears a gallant costume of silk, either purple, green, blue, or pink, composed of knee-breeches embroidered with silver trimmings, light silk stockings, a jacket also adorned with elaborate trimmings in silver, and a bright-hued sash ; his hair is worn in a *chignon*, and besides his long sword he carries a red cloak with which to beguile the bull. The picadores, who are mounted and armed with spears, come next in rank to the espada. They wear short velvet jackets of vivid colors, splendidly embroidered, gaudy vests, and frilled shirts, cravats of mixed colors loosely knotted, silken sashes, buffalo-hide trousers over a light armor which is designed to protect the legs from the bull's horns, wide-brimmed *sombreros* of gray. The duty of these big fellows is to prod the bull while he is engaged in goring their horses to death. The banderilleros, who are arrayed like the espada, only not quite so sumptuously, are on foot, and have to plant barbs in the bull's neck. The chulos, by the use of their red cloaks, draw the bull's attention here and there as the exigency may require. Then

there are a lot of men in red caps, called *miradores*,
a kind of " supers," who find plenty of occupation in
stripping the saddles and bridles off from dying
horses, stopping the wounds of other steeds with
plugs of cotton, in order that they may serve once
more, and kindred pleasant services. All these
functionaries would look supremely absurd in such
gorgeous costumes if it were not for the fact that they
are superbly built men, of elegant carriage and great
dignity of demeanor.

When the bull enters the ring, he finds two mounted
picadores and a half-dozen or more chulos there. He
usually kills the two horses (unless he is a very
cowardly specimen) and as many more as he has the
courage to gore in the space of ten minutes or there-
about, — for as fast as the picadores are unhorsed they
are supplied with fresh steeds. Of course the moment
a horse is down, the chulos draw the bull away by
flirting their cloaks in front of him, so that the picador
has time to get out of the way in safety. Nevertheless
the picadores are often hurt, and a spare hand is
always in waiting to replace the wounded man — also,
by the way, a surgeon and a priest. At the end of
a short space of time the governor gives a signal,
trumpets sound, and the picadores retire to give place
to the banderilleros, two in number, who each try to
place a couple of pairs of barbs in the bull's neck (a
dangerous feat), which is often done so deftly that it
is impossible to see the man's motions. The bander-

illeros are called off by the trumpet-signal presently, and the espada comes to the front. He makes a little speech to the governor, which means that he intends to do his whole duty, etc., flings his cap on the

ground, and approaches the bull with his sword hid under the folds of a short red cloak. After playing with the animal a while, he kills him by a single thrust in a vital spot, plunging the Toledo blade in its entire length. The bull then usually staggers a few steps, falls on his knees, and in a few moments rolls over on his side.

Six or eight bulls are commonly sacrificed in one corrida. Of course they vary in character, so that no two combats are alike. The best bulls are bred in Andalusia, it is said; but, as it happened, the liveliest animal I saw was one of the six in Burgos. He was enormous in size and magnificently built; and when he entered the ring he did not stop in the centre to look around as some bulls do, but he went for the nearest picador like a shot, and lifted the horse on his horns two or three feet from the ground, amid a tempest of cheers. By the time that horse came down

to the earth in his death agony, rolling and kicking so
that the picador was in great peril, the plucky bull had
crossed the arena on a run, sending chulos one after
another skipping over the fence for safety, and had
impaled the second horse, whose rider gracefully
alighted on the fence and escaped being crushed. So
for ten minutes this bull, never for a moment on the
defensive, sent one horse after another into the eternity

of hacks, until eight dead and dying horses were lying
on the ground, and the audience was almost frantic
with delight and admiration. I found myself wiping
the cold perspiration from my brow, and (I may as
well confess it) before long I was jumping up and
down and shouting as lustily as any of them. However, no man was hurt. This go-ahead sort of bull is
less feared, they say, than the slow and sly kind. The

sympathy of the audience is invariably on the side of pluck wherever it is shown, either in bull or man ; the element of fair play is left out, however, for the odds are all in the favor of the men.

The vocabulary of tauromachy is voluminous, and in Madrid the newspaper reports of a combat are as packed with the slang of the ring as a report of a base-ball match in America is full of " hot liners," " muffs," " first-base hits," " foul tips," and the like. The popular admiration for an expert espada can hardly be overstated. If he despatches the bull artistically, he is wildly cheered, and as he struts around the ring to acknowledge the throng's plaudits, the excited spectators throw cigars, fans, hats, and all sorts of objects to the ground before him. He picks up and keeps the cigars and fans, and gravely tosses back the hats. By the time the corrida is over, the sun has nearly set, and it is past the dinner-hour. Exhausted by excitement, the spectators go straight from this scene of blood and death to their quiet homes, — polished gentlemen, gentle ladies, and even little children, — where they sit down to their dinner, amid a fine perfume of the adjacent mule-stable, and talk over the events of the day.

To see a horse wantonly killed, no matter how worthless a rawboned hack he may be, is no fun, but apart from that feature of the sport, a bull-fight is thoroughly enjoyable, and after the first shock is past there is a peculiar and exceptional fascination about it.

There is nothing like it! The story is told of a certain American who saw his first bull-fight, in Madrid, in 1881, and was made quite sick by the sight of so much blood. He went away with his nerves unstrung and his appetite for beef gone. In order to efface the disagreeable impression he retired to the country for a few days, after expressing his abhorrence for the brutality of the Spaniards in no measured terms. On the following Sunday he turned up again at the Plaza de Toros, and sat through the whole performance, which he probably enjoyed immensely. We went twice, — the second time in Madrid. There was less sport there, however, than there had been in Burgos. The bulls were not so lively, and the audience was less demonstrative.

CHAPTER V.

THERE are 230 rivers in Spain according to one authority. The Arlanzon, at Burgos, is a fair sample of the great majority of these streams, whose names and whose bridges are so much more impressive in size than themselves. Along the bank of the Arlanzon is the public promenade, called the Espolon, which, on the evening of the festival, was lighted by many hundreds of Chinese lanterns, the paper exteriors of which had an unfortunate aptitude for taking fire and burning up. There was a great throng of well-behaved people abroad. The two bridges were illuminated, as well as the promenade, and the long lines of colored lights made a very pleasant effect. Many little "shows" were in progress in tents and booths, and there was great animation and much entertainment for the stranger whichever way he turned. The men smoked cigarettes, and the women talked, incessantly. This agreeable evening scene did something towards effacing the unpleasant impression Burgos had made upon us: but — however promptly one forgets many of the bothers of travel after they are past — my nose will long remind me of the fragrant metropolis of Old Castile!

The distance from Burgos to Madrid is 363 kilometres by rail. The express-train makes the run in about eight hours, and the first-class fare is about $9. Nothing more desolate can be imagined than the region through which you pass. Vast plains, almost devoid of vegetation and totally without a tree of any kind, huge gaunt ridges and isolated peaks of bare rock, great basins and val-leys stretching as far as the eye can reach, sere and scorched, encumbered with thousands of gray bowlders, but never containing a village, a tree, a blade of grass, or a stream of water, — nothing to relieve the sight. For hour after hour the train toils tediously along through this lonesome, forsaken, and unspeakably dreary expanse. The sun pours into the carriage relentlessly; not a breath of air can be felt; the passengers fan themselves and at each station get out and drink huge glasses of water. Sometimes it seems as if the train would never start again; at one station it stops fifteen minutes; at another, half an hour; at a third, a full hour; and these long stops are apparently without cause. No

one knows why the train does not go on, and the
passengers do not seem to care particularly, or, at all
events, they are so well used to this sort of thing that
they take it as a matter of course; nothing surprises
them.   They all have baskets, bags, or bundles full
of bread, cheese, cold meats, fruit, wine, etc., for they
know it would be suicide to depend on arriving at a
station where there is a *buffet* at any given hour.   But
the Spaniards are light eaters in any case, and do not
give much thought to the subject of food.   They are
accustomed to miserable fare, and would not appreciate
anything better.   A more patient people does not
exist.   They are never in a hurry, and, if you are, so
much the worse for you.

Before reaching Madrid the railway crosses the Sierra
Guadarrama and passes from Old, into New, Castile.
These mountains furnish snow all summer with which
to quench the eternal thirst of the Madrid people, who
use the snow in lieu of ice in their beverages.

CHAPTER VI.

MADRID.

You are told that the capital is one of the most uninteresting towns in the whole country. The people of the old Andalusian cities, and the thrifty Catalans, despise the "mushroom metropolis." Much that is said  against Madrid may be true, but then — the picture-gallery is there! The other cities may point to the glories of the past, but the Museo is a glory of to-day and unites the proud past of Spain with her future possibilities. Madrid is, it may be admitted, less distinctively Spanish in character than the other large cities, and for that very reason it is in many respects a more comfortable place of residence. It has the best hôtels in Spain, and modern comforts and conveniences can be had by paying for them. The Fonda de la Paz indeed is, though expensive, the only first-rate hôtel in Spain, unless the accounts of travelers are untrustworthy. It has almost the American system. You pay so much *per diem* for your room and your three meals, and there is a " secretary," who comes very near the American hôtel " clerk " (only he is not so proud or so patronizing), and who is quite

constantly on hand in the office to answer inquiries
and attend to the needs of the guests.

It was very warm, and on our arrival we were
exceedingly tired, hungry, and travel-stained. The
large, airy room, with closely barred shutters, and a
couple of inviting high beds, looked like a vision of
paradise to our jaded sight. The servant brought a
perfumed bath, a delicious Oriental luxury, which was
fully appreciated; and presently we were seated on
a well-shaded little balcony overlooking the gay and
glaring Puerta del Sol, drinking huge draughts of one
of those marvelous cooling beverages known only to
Madrid, and feeling rejuvenated. At the dinner-table
there was a still greater surprise for us in the shape
of a very tolerable imitation of a French bill-of-fare,
and the waiters spoke French. An acrid red wine
was served, which appeared to inflame rather than allay
the thirst. There were several French people in the
dining-room, whom I took to be commercial travelers,
except one couple, who, if appearances are not wholly
deceitful, were in the theatrical line. I wonder if
every one who has sojourned at this particular hôtel
in Madrid has as distinct a recollection of that dining-
room, and of the little reading-room adjoining it, as I
have! For it was there that we heard of the assassi-
nation of President Garfield. We were taking our
after-dinner cup of black coffee, and looking over the
journals, when the secretary came in, and knowing us
to be Americans, said to us, in French, that an attempt

had been made upon the life of the President of the United States. We treated it as a hoax. But the evening newspapers, loudly announced by shrill-voiced newsboys through the great square, confirmed the ugly tidings, and later in the evening word came that the President was dead. Would that he had died then, and been spared that hideous summer of pain! Whenever a word of hostility towards Spain rises to my lips, I think of the manly sympathy of the Spanish people as expressed by hundreds of them at that time, and I leave the word unspoken. They said, with pride, that King Alfonso had been the first to send a message of condolence to Washington. It was pleasant to attribute much of the kindly interest shown by the Spaniards then to a latent sympathy with democratic institutions.

The King, by the way, was in town, so that we could not see the interior of the royal palace, which, according to all accounts, does not contain much to interest the sight-seer. His Majesty was to be seen every afternoon riding out with a modest retinue. He goes to the monastery of Atocha often to attend religious services. He is said to be a liberal-minded monarch, and takes a great interest in all subjects pertaining to the welfare of the people. He reads the daily papers of all shades of opinion with a regularity which speaks well for his industry, and it should be borne in mind that the journals are as outspoken as you please, for the press is practically free. The Prince of Wales gracefully called Alfonso "a model king," on the occasion of his visit to Spain a few years ago. The favorite language in the palace is German, in deference to the Queen, but the King speaks French and English also. Royalty has ever been accomplished in a linguistic way. We had the pleasure of meeting General Fairchild, then United States Minister to Spain, who exerted himself to render our sojourn in Madrid agreeable. He took us to the beautiful garden of the Buen Retiro, where we met Señor Castellar, the stanch republican, the scholar, orator, and statesman, who was the friend of Charles Sumner. With admirable good sense and loyalty, this great man, who compels the respect of political adversaries, supports cheerfully the present government, believing that the time for a republic will come sooner or later, but holding it a crime to lift a hand against a fellow-citizen in behalf of no matter how beautiful a theory.

In how great need has Spain been for many generations past of this kind of unselfish patriotism! She has lost countless men in civil war, rebellion, and revolution, and it is only since the quite recent suppression of the Carlist war that the country has had time to take breath and count up her losses. Already industry is reviving, and confidence, a plant of slow growth, beginning to be restored. All that the country needs is peace, stability, and the consequent chance to recover lost gound. Seville, Malaga, and Barcelona are growing rapidly, and extending their commercial relations on every hand. In Andalusia improved agricultural machinery has been introduced with gratifying results. The politicians, angry and jealous over the French and English conquests in Africa, are casting hungry eyes towards Morocco; there is no reason why Spain should not have a slice of the African pie. It would give the young bloods in the army something to do.

The army, which has always been the too ready tool of revolutionists and political intriguers, is said to be no longer available for such purposes. "The soldiers will not fire on Spaniards," said a Sevillian to me. "If a general is found intriguing nowadays, he is taken out and made an example of at short notice."

General Fairchild agreed with Castellar, and with almost every intelligent person, that the advent of the republican régime is only a question of time, that it is bound to come, but that it will not do to hurry it, for the people are in need still of more or less preparation for the grave responsibility of self-government.

Madrid apes the fashions of Paris, and is flattered to be considered a good imitation of the French capital (which she is not), just as Brussels calls herself the "little Paris," and as Cincinnati is willing to be esteemed the "Paris of America." Imitations are but poor things at best. Whatever is really of the most value in a town, as in other things, must be original. The cafés of Madrid are numerous, and a few of them, especially on the Puerta del Sol, the Calle de Alcalá,

and the Carrera de San Gerónimo, are large and
elegant.   Besides the cafés, there are *cerbezerias*
(beer-halls), *tavernas* (ordinary bars), and *horchate-
rias*, where they deal exclusively in the wonderful
summer drink, the *horchata de chufas*, a sweet, barley-
water mixture, the color of muddy milk, with snow in
it.   It is very wholesome in hot weather, but it is too
sweet to suit most palates. A more attractive beverage
is *cerbeza con limon*, beer mixed with lemon juice,
which is brewed, ice-cold, in a large punchbowl, and
quenches thirst excellently.   Then there is *agraz*,
described as " clarified verjus," and highly recommended by Ford ; but I could never get it at any of
the first-class cafés.   The first time I ordered it, the
waiter brought me a glass of coffee ; the second time
a cup of very thick chocolate.   I was afraid to make
any further experiments with the language, and
desisted.   The Spanish wines, high as their reputation
is, are seldom found palatable in Spain.   All the best
sherry is exported, and the same may be said for the
Malaga and Tarragona wines.   The red wines are
sharp, and inflame thirst.   In the South they have on
the hôtel tables a white wine, tasting like watered
sherry.   The best standard table wine is the Valde-
peñas, and perhaps also the Manzanilla.

The lower classes drink a great deal of *agua-ardi-
ente*, which may be described as " fire-water."   It has
an aromatic taste, far from disagreeable, and turns
a cloudy white when mixed with water.   The depraved

associations evoked by this subject lead me to speak of tobacco. Don't go to Spain, O slave of the weed! supposing that because Cuba is a Spanish possession you can get Havana cigars there. Nine tenths of all the Havana cigars go to the United States; but in revenge you can smoke cigarettes made of Virginia tobacco in Spain. They are rather bad cigarettes, and the cigars to be got in the *estancos* are not much better, as a rule. Occasionally a three-cent cigar may turn out to be very good, but the expensive ones are invariably bad.

Fruit Vender, MADRID.

The Puerta del Sol is by all odds the most interesting part of Madrid. A large proportion of the population spends its days and nights on the broad sidewalks, talking and laughing and moving to and fro, — soldiers, priests, bull-fighters, and women, — a motley crowd. All is animation. The fountain throws up its jet of water ceaselessly in the centre of the big square, the horse-cars come and go in four different directions, carriages dash here and there, the newsboys and match-venders keep up an endless racket, and above all rises the murmur of a thousand voices. What are they all talking about?

The Prado is the park. As soon as the sun goes

down everybody starts for the Prado, which includes
the Retiro, or fashionable drive, the Salon, where
swells afoot and on horseback air themselves, and the
charming garden of the Buen Retiro.   On the Retiro
you may see, from half-past six till eight o'clock,
a great throng of fine equipages, four abreast, the
whole length of the drive.   The Salon is a sort of
second-class Champs Elysées, a shadowy reminder of
the great Parisian avenue.   A broad gravel walk is
bordered by rows of iron chairs, in which one may sit
(for a consideration) and look at the promenaders who
pass and repass at a sedate gait.   As for the Buen
Retiro, it is a pretty garden with trees, shrubbery,
winding pathways, zinc palms, colored lights, stirring
band music, out-door variety-shows, vaudevilles, and
ballets, — in fact, a respectable Jardin Mabille, patronized by good society, and the only place to spend
a summer evening in, for of course the theatres are
mostly closed.   It is in such a place, too, that you may
see the Madrilenians as they are at home.   They are
certainly a good-looking and well-behaved people.   A
few of the women have begun to wear hats and
bonnets in place of the lace tocas which are so becoming, — a sad mistake on their part.

Of course we went to see the royal armory and the
royal stables.   The first contains I know not how
many suits of armor worn by Christian and Moorish
heroes of old : for that is one of those things I cannot get excited over, though the guidebook call on me

ever so loudly for appropriate emotions. The stables are of great interest, however, for even a republican may admire the aristocratic qualities of a horse of high pedigree, and there is no end to the blooded pets of Alfonso's equine palace. They are English, French, Arabian, — a splendid lot of mettlesome fellows, who probably don't get enough exercise. The carriages are very numerous and sumptuous, but all except those of American make seem unneccessarily heavy and clumsy.

There is one particular in which Madrid is peculiar, and stands alone among European cities: she has no churches which the most frenzied tourist would wish to visit. This gives her a certain pre-eminence which no other feature could confer.

CHAPTER VII.

THE PICTURE-GALLERY.

UNTIL within a few years the Royal Museum of the Prado has been almost unknown beyond the borders of Spain. The immense value of the collection is beginning to be generally appreciated, but it remains the most unfamiliar among the really great galleries of Europe. It is called less complete, chronologically, than the Louvre, and so it is ; but as a collection of masterpieces it is unsurpassed in the world, and no other collection except that of the Louvre can for one moment be compared with it. Indeed I have heard artists say that even the Louvre looked rather tame to them after they had visited Madrid. Apart from the significant fact that nowhere else can an adequate idea be gained concerning the Spanish school, the collection is extremely rich in its Italian and Dutch departments. The great room known as the Salon of Queen Isabella contains the principal masterpieces of all the schools, without distinction, and I doubt if there is another roomfull like it in the world.

The gallery is in the Prado, and is approached from the centre of the town through the Carrera de San Gerónimo, where is the palace of the Cortes — a handsome building — and an interesting statue of

Cervantes. An excellent catalogue, in French, exists, and on weekdays there is a nominal admittance fee of ten cents, but on Sundays the galleries are free. The large central hall is well-lighted from the top, but the side rooms are ill-lighted, and should be seen at certain hours when the light is best. The Spanish school must first claim our attention. As for numbers, there are sixty-four examples of Velasquez, forty-six of Murillo, fifty-eight of Ribera, fourteen of Zurbarán, eighteen of Macip, or (Joanés), a roomfull of Goya's paintings, and a considerable number by Cano.

If we take Murillo, Velasquez, Ribera, Goya, and the rest of the famous Spanish painters for true exponents of the national characteristics, many preconceived notions must be upset ; these are a most saturnine, sober, sad folk. Their pleasures are grotesque and fierce, their humor impish and rough. An undercurrent of gloom runs through all their merry-making, as a barbaric minor strain is heard in the midst of their gayest music.

Velasquez is very justly the favorite of painters. So full of the subtle modern flavor are his works, that it is hard to realize that he died more than two centuries ago. No man ever made a more abrupt " new departure " in the way of looking at things. The Spaniards always painted as literally as they knew how, even the most ideal of subjects, but they were rigidly formal, and only copied the weaknesses of the Italians, their native strength running to brutality and

harshness. It remained for Velasquez to combine
force with refinement, and freedom with firmness, after
his own manner. It would be almost impossible to
convey a satisfactory idea of his very numerous paintings monopolized by this gallery. His portraits are
superb for their vigor, genuineness, and *verve*, the
absence of any trickery or superficiality. They have
a truly patrician flavor, like Van Dyck's portraits, and
such as is eminently appropriate in the likenesses of
royal heirs, kings, and princesses of high degree; but
their greatest charm is inexplicable, as is always the
case with the best works of art. Simplicity and sincerity, with great learning and skill of hand — that is
all there is of Velasquez. "The Topers" ("Los Bebedores") is as marvelous a specimen of technical perfection as any of his works. It is one of those pictures
in front of which an artist halts and makes confession
that he does not know how to paint. Conviviality was
never represented with greater truth or humor. The
spirit of Bacchus is over all the scene. It is full of
human nature in its pagan aspect, rollicking in the joy
of exuberant physical life. It is a drinking-song in
color, a "rouse," a jolly "time," anything but a temperance tract. Still its humor saves it from grossness.
Velasquez was incapable of vulgarity. On the contrary, he could paint nobility in a dwarf, and give
dignity to commonplace figures. The picture of "The
Spinners," a splendid composition, representing
women at work in a large weaving-room, is worthy to

be rated equal with "The Topers," and Mengs said of it, very happily, that it seemed as if it had been the work of pure thought. "Las Meniñas" ("The Maids of Honor") is one of the most celebrated of this happy man's works. "O, if I could only paint like that, I would be satisfied to leave one such picture to the world!" said an artist. It represents Velasquez himself in his studio, as he was painting the portrait of the charming little Infanta Maria Margarita, whose maids are grouped about her. There are eight or ten figures, and on the walls are pictures which are said to have been Rubens's. The composition is full of historic interest. Sir W. Stirling Maxwell, in a capital description of it, gives the names of all the characters, and many entertaining details. "The dresses," he says, "are highly absurd, their figures being concealed by long stiff corsets and prodigious hoops." But who, once having seen the picture, would wish it to be otherwise in any particular? The King, and Giordano the Italian, who was at that period painting in Madrid, conspired to make "Las Meniñas" one of the most famous paintings of all time: the former, by seizing a brush and painting the Cross of Santiago upon the breast of the figure of Velasquez, the latter, by calling the picture the "theology of painting." Both compliments were remarkable, though the latter has more sound than sense, but nothing ever turned Velasquez's head; he was used to royal favors, and probably knew he deserved them. He has made Philip IV's face and figure familiar to posterity in all sorts of becoming expressions, attitudes, and costumes, and it is easy to imagine how delightful as a loafing-place the monarch found his studio. It is not my intention to speak in detail of the famous " Capture of Breda " (" Las Lanzas"), or of " Vulcan's Forge." Among the portraits there is not one which is not interesting as a faithful description of a real person, from that of the blithe little Prince Balthazar-Charles, who rides his pot-bellied pony with such easy grace, to.the picture of the most grotesque dwarf in Philip's court. The *quality* is always there, and can be felt. It is the rarest talent to paint portraits well. There are so many bad portraits in the world! — so many libels on individuals, and so many caricatures of humanity in general, — no wonder that Eugène Fromentin can count on his fingers the great portraitists of the world.* The men of to-day are turning to Velasquez to see what he can teach them in the province of portrait-painting. And they are right. Bonnat and Carolus Durah are well enough in their way, but they themselves, if frankly asked for advice, would say to the young men, " Go to the fountain-heads. The Louvre is better than the Salon. The old masters knew how better than the best of us." None of them had what Fromentin calls " cette naïveté attentive, soumise et forte," which the study of the human face

---

* Titian, Rembrandt, Raphael, Sebastian del Piombo, Velasquez, Van Dyck, Holbein, Antoine More.

requires in order to be perfect, in so great a degree as Velasquez. Only a painter can appreciate such triumphs as " Los Bebedores " and " Las Meniñas." Velasquez's genuis was more robustly masculine than that of Murillo, but if it excels in force, directness, and accurate brilliancy of characterization, it lacks the sweet and almost feminine quality of the other's religious compositions. His realism is always of the refined sort, never brutal, never pretentious. He has an intensely original and distinguished style. By looking at any one of his portraits, one can guess his personal refinement, his cultivated mind, his rectitude and strength of character. His taste was never at fault. His intelligence never forsook him. His manual skill was equal to the immense demands made upon it. He had his materials apparently under perfect control, or as nearly so as may be. And he not only controlled his means : he controlled his subject also. His model never entirely ran away with him ; he always managed to work in a little of Velasquez. His observation was more developed than his imagination, but his insight was keen, he analyzed people and things with a good deal of penetration, and as he was well-off, healthy, and happy, his art is sane, alert, cheerful. In this regard he was different from all his contemporaries, and remains unique.

Murillo, with less command of technique, had the soft heart of a woman, and the capacity of feeling the spiritual anguish of the Virgin as few painters ever did

before or since. No sceptic could look upon one of
the two great "Immaculate Conceptions," in the main
gallery, without a deep respect (to say the least) for the
motive of the work as well as for the lovable human
qualities of the painter who could thus portray the
sweetness and innocence of womanhood. I am aware
that Murillo has been placed in the second rank of artists
by Ruskin and some other critics ; but I doubt if they
were familiar with his best works when they so unjustly
estimated him. The big "Assumption," in the Louvre,
does not represent him at his highest level, though it
is one of his "important" canvases. One of the two
large paintings of the same subject in the Madrid
gallery is so entirely apart from the conventional Virgin,
whose meek expression and upturned eyes are so
often reproduced, that it seems at first almost an
infraction of the unwritten laws governing ecclesiastical
art. There is a human air about it, and presently you
begin to feel that if there exists a Holy Virgin you
have now seen her real self. Not that there is less of
innocence and tenderness and sanctified beauty in this
case — but a more human type, and a younger, fresher,
and more recognizable countenance brings the mystery
closer to you. This is a much better work in conception, if not in execution, than the "Immaculate Conception," in the Square Hall of the Louvre. There is
more character in the face of the Virgin, though I
cannot agree with those who find the other insipid and
commonplace. In his love of the beautiful, and in his

grace, religious **earnestness and** tenderness, Murillo was pre-eminent, — how completely so can hardly be appreciated without visiting both Madrid **and Seville.** In the "Divine Shepherd" is a beautiful **type of** guileless childhood, with much of the quality of *naïveté*, both in the character of the subject and in its treatment. The same quality is seen in the "Christ and St. John." The great picture of the "Vision of Saint Anthony of Padua" is in Seville, **and I** shall speak of it further on. The Academy **of** Arts and Sciences in Madrid possesses **several** of Murillo's **most** esteemed paintings, one of which, "St. Elizabeth" dressing the sores **of the poor,** is called his greatest **work;** it is a very marvelous canvas, and technically perhaps his greatest performance, but the **subject is** most repulsive.

Ribera was **a very strong** painter in **every** respect, and in **spite of his** long residence in Italy, his works are particularly national, **and are** valuable for their illustration of marked Spanish tendencies. He was **predisposed to** take the tragic view, **and** liked to **depict** such episodes and subjects as the flaying **of St.** Bartholomew, Ixion **on the** wheel, etc. Some of his works are unutterably gloomy and dark, both in color and motive. In his "Prometheus" he shows you the blood and intestines of the victim, painted with revolting fidelity. His "Jacob's Ladder," in the salon of Queen Isabella, is considered his greatest work, and it is, in fact, remarkable in expressional power. **But the most impressive example of** this master, who **was said** to employ every means to crush out his rivals, not hesitating at murder, is a representation of the " Holy Trinity." A beautiful and venerable head is that of the Father, a calm, sad old man with white hair, an ample beard, and a Roman nose. This head is projected against a luminous space in the centre of a cloudy background. Below is the crucified Son, his head falling back on the Father's knee, his arms outstretched, and the lower part of his body, which is modeled with exceptional power, is borne up by a sheet held by cherubs. The deathly pallor of his countenance, the gaping wound in his side, and the rigidity of his limbs, expressed marvelously, contribute to the feeling of painful truth which is conveyed by this great work. Just above the head of the Christ is a white dove with outstretched wings representing the Holy Spirit.

But Goya even surpassed Ribera in his realistic descriptions of horrible events and scenes. His works are set apart in a special room, and are supposed to form a complete exposition of the strangely picturesque manners and customs of the Spaniards. Gautier gives a charming chapter about this odd genius. He painted with sticks, brooms, sponges — any tool that served his purpose, and " donnait les touches de sentiment à grands coups de pouce."* His " Second of May," which represented French soldiers massacring

---

* Though there is nothing new about this except the phrase " touches de sentiment," which is intensely Gautieresque.

the Spanish inhabitants, is said to have been blocked
in with a spoon. He was a violent satirist, and set
forth the fanaticism, gluttony, and stupidity of the
monks, the ignorance and vices of the courtiers, the
follies of polite society, with extraordinary and malignant force. His ideal caprices are like the nightmares
produced by a morbid fancy, and are frightful beyond
description. His pictures of bull-fights are numerous,
and marked by an exceedingly impressive compound
of realism and strange conceits. He painted many
war-scenes, as horrible as the most unbridled imagination could make them. An erratic cynicism pervaded
all his works, which exercise a certain grim fascination
over the mind of the spectator. He painted portraits
very well, and his equestrian portraits of Charles IV
and his wife are admirable serious works. A portrait
of Goya himself, by Lopez, shows him to have been
a broad-faced old gentleman, whose good-humored and
well-fed appearance is quite at variance with the idea
of him gained from a contemplation of his works.
Alonso Cano is fairly represented in the gallery by
a picture of the Virgin worshiping her Son, and a
" Dead Christ Mourned by Angels"; but we shall see
more of him in his native city of Granada, where he
was equally renowned as a painter and sculptor. Cano,
like Ribera, had the reputation of putting out of the
way people whom he did not like. He was accused of
murdering his wife. It seems to have been quite the
fashion among the seventeenth-century Spanish artists

to remove in a summary manner all real or fancied
obstacles to their success.

After this outline survey of the Spanish masters,
who at least make a stranger feel some respect for
their country, let us take a look at the Italians. Think
of forty-three Titians!   What a glorious collection !
It is indescribable.   The schools of Venice, Florence,
Rome, Parma, Bologna, Naples, — all are represented ;
but the chief strength lies in the great Venetian school
with its forty-three Titians, its thirty-four Tintorets,
its twenty-five Paul Veroneses, and its crowd of Del
Piombos, Malombras, and Tiepolos.   Then, for the
other schools, there is Raphael with ten examples of
prime importance, Guido Reni with sixteen canvases,
Luca Giordano with sixty-six, and an uneven but
strongly interesting lot of Da Vincis, Del Sartos,
Correggios, and the rest.   Among the ten canvases
by Raphael is the holy family known as " The Pearl."
It was so named by Philip IV.   It was formerly owned
by Charles I of England, and was disposed of by
Cromwell with the rest of the royal rubbish.   It
brought $10,000 at that time.   If at present $200,000
is asked for the Raphael exhibited in New York, what
would " The Pearl" not be worth to our famishing
museums at that rate of valuation ? Then there is the
same master's " Spasimo di Sicilia," representing Jesus
succumbing under the weight of the cross and sus-
tained by Simon ; the " Visitation," representing St.
Elizabeth and the Virgin ; the well-known Madonnas

of the Fish and of the Rose ; with his Holy Family of
the Lamb and his portrait of the Cardinal Julius de
Medici. Titian's " Offering to the Goddess of Love,"
an ill-balanced composition, is remarkable for its crowd
of hilarious and beautiful infants ; but there is nothing
more captivating than his portraits, the portrait of
himself for instance, or the famous portraits of Charles
V on foot and on horseback. In fact the number of
really great portraits in the Madrid gallery is astonish-
ing. Some of Titian's best works are here, and there
are none better. The model for his Salomé, who
bears the head of John the Baptist on a charger, was
his daughter Lavinia.

The Dutch and Flemish department is quite as
remarkable as one would expect to find it, even in
the national gallery of Spain. There are sixty-six
examples of Rubens, twenty-two of Van Dyck, fifty-
five of Teniers, fifty-four of Breughel, and a few of
Rembrandt's, Jordaens's, Wouvermans's, and Bosch's
works, forming a priceless collection. The representation of Rubens is superior to that in the Louvre,
and includes some of his most fleshly creations, — once
modestly stowed away in the basement, but now displayed in the main gallery. They are superb, these
human animals of his, and appeal to all that is pagan
in the most civilized Christian nature. The humor in
Teniers's group of six paintings, depicting monkeys
dressed in the costumes of men, and engaged in eating,
drinking, smoking, playing at school, and aping the

postures and expressions of painters and sculptors, is
simply irresistible. How stirring are the breezy hunt-
ing-scenes of Wouvermans, how fresh and gallant his
figures of cavaliers and dames, who sweep gayly down
a slope in pursuit of some unseen hare! I remember
particularly one of these scenes which impressed me
with all the newness and joy of a spring morning, a
sense of the immense happiness of living, and of
being young; yet I do not remember the composition
itself with sufficient distinctness to describe it. It was
merely the flavor and the gusto of the thing. Some
of Van Dyck's most spirited and patrician portraits are
here; among them those of the Duchess of Oxford,
of the artist himself, and his patron, the Count of
Bristol, of Liberti, the organist of Antwerp, of the
Prince of Orange, Henry of Nassau, of Henry, Count
of Bergh, and of the painter David Ryckaert. For
the full-lengths Van Dyck used to ask $300! Our
modern portrait-painters are not so badly off as they
think, after all. A head of Christ, wearing the crown
of thorns, is the only serious work, setting aside the
portraits, which can be called powerful and original;
it is thoroughly manly in character, — one of the
strongest and least diluted of Van Dyck's works.

In the French room there is not much that is
remarkable. Good specimens of Poussin, Claude,
David, Watteau, Ingres, Largillière, are to be seen, but
many great names are missing. There are twenty
Poussins and ten Claudes. One of the Claudes

("Paysage, la Madeleine à genoux, le matin") is well worthy to be hung where it is, among the rarest masterpieces in the Queen's salon, for, though very much blackened by age, it is a perfect example of the sombre and mysterious classical landscape at its best, making the beholder dream of grand old forests and cool shadows and glimpses of an infinitely remote sky, just touched by the first faint reflections of the dawn, long after he has passed the smoky old canvas and departed from the silent gallery.

There may be more complete, more symmetrical collections of pictures, but there can be none better. It was a long time before we could tear ourselves away from Madrid. Every morning by common consent we turned our steps towards the Museo, and spent many long and blissful hours there, till our eyes ached, and our spinal columns cried out for a rest. And how many times since have we, in memory, wandered through these enchanted halls, recalling each favorite picture, and renewing the purest pleasures of a lifetime!

ANDALUSIA is represented to be an earthly paradise. Its climate in July is such as we are accustomed to associate with an entirely different locality. The journey from Madrid to Seville occupies fourteen hours, and is best taken at night. The express-train goes three times a week. Leaving Madrid at six o'clock P. M., after an unusually early dinner, you are enabled to see all that you wish to see of La Mancha, the scene of some of Don Quixote's adventures,* an indescribably dreary desert, in comparison with which even the gaunt and forlorn

* Mr. Waterman calls his illustration "A Veritable Spanish Windmill." This has reference to Gustave Doré's spurious Spanish windmills, which are of an entirely different pattern.

wastes of New Castile are cheerful and luxuriant. It is literally true, as Washington Irving says, that it is "a stern, melancholy country, with rugged mountains and long, sweeping plains, destitute of trees and indescribably silent and lonesome, partaking of the savage and solitary character of Africa." But there is no longer any spice of danger from banditti, as there was fifty-odd years ago, when Irving made his romantic pilgrimage to the Alhambra. The great heat, the miserable food, the tormenting fleas, the nauseating odors, and the importunate beggars cannot be dignified under the name of dangers, and there is nothing romantic about the railway-trains of Spain, be they ever so slow. At nine in the evening the train halts at the station of Alcazar de San Juan, and the passengers indulge in the chocolate and sponge-cake for which the place is renowned. After this harmless lunch the traveler settles himself for the night, and is lulled to sleep by the monotonous motion and rattle of the train. There are no sleeping-cars on the lines south of Madrid, but there are expensive reclining-chairs, or what the French call *fauteuil-lits*. It is generally safe for men to trust to luck for a couple of seats in a first-class carriage, where the human form divine can be extended nearly at full length, and the hand-bag or bundle of wraps utilized as a pillow. It is best not to say much about the personal appearance in the morning of the individual who sleeps in this way. At six A. M., the train comes to a standstill in Cordova, and there is

time to get out and take a cup of so-called coffee.
The exquisite maiden who so bewitched the susceptible
De Amicis at this ancient place has departed. She lives
in Burgos now, I believe. Cordova from the railway

looks very sleepy and insignificant in the early morning, — a stretch of low, white walls, with square towers
here and there, and the Græco-Roman tower of the
cathedral dominating the town. The train now follows
the course of the Guadalquivir, and runs alongside of
immense hedges of rank, dusty cactus, and one catches
glimpses of strange southern forms of vegetation
formerly unknown ; for we are fairly in the marvelous
beau pays of which we have read so much. But though
Andalusia is described with so much vague enthusiasm,
it is a beau pays only in comparison with the ugly
interior provinces. Near Seville, the train passes
through a long succession of extensive olive plantations.
As a shade-tree the olive-tree is not a success, but it is
better than nothing. The foliage is dusty and pale,
and the trees have a stunted and forlorn appearance ;

they are planted in regular rows, and the berries, which are not gathered until towards winter, are almost all made into oil. At all the stations big placards freshly posted up announced a grand bull-fight of extraordinary interest at Malaga the following Sunday. Espadas and picadores from Madrid, Seville, Cordova, and other towns were to participate; bulls from Señor ——'s breeding-farm would be introduced; and excursion-trains were to be run from several distant points. These posters excited no small degree of interest on the part of the passengers, who read and reread them and then discussed the prospects. It was growing frightfully hot, and the courteous *caballeros* in our coupé began to discard garment after garment, until we became anxious least they should be entirely nude by the time we arrived in Seville. But no such thrilling incident happened. We are at last in the gay Andalusian metropolis, at nine o'clock of a blistering, scalding day, and — O joy! — the porter of the Four Nations Hôtel has captured us with a few words of pigeon-English which we are too tired to resist.

"You have come off Madrid?" he says, after rescuing the trunk, expanding his mouth in a sociable smile.

"Yes."

"Ah! You are English?"

"No."

"Ah! You are Americans?"

"Yes."

The clever José is pleased with his own penetration,
and continues to talk all the way up to the hôtel, which
is on a great square full of tall palm-trees, where three
consolidated bands give concerts on summer evenings.
After the intolerable heat of the streets, the marble-

paved *patio* of the hôtel seems a deliciously cool and
pleasant spot.   The men sitting about are smoking
cigarettes, drinking coffee, reading the papers a little,
loafing, and gossiping, without the slightest pretense
of doing anything more fatiguing than to draw the
breath of life.   We are shown to a room by the ener-
getic José, and after a bite of breakfast we proceed to
make ourselves as comfortable as the circumstances
will permit — for the thermometer indicates a degree
of heat equal to 98° Fahrenheit.   The process is quite

simple: we remove all our clothes except our shirts, and sit with our feet in basins full of water. A cigar and a French novel — say by Cherbuliez — make the arrangement complete. There is a monotonous hum of female voices just outside the door, where a group of women are sitting at their needlework in the corridor, and the intermittent music of a guitar floats from some unseen patio; so presently we fall asleep. Thus we pass our first day in Seville.

CHAPTER IX

SEVILLE.

SEVILLE is undoubtedly the most Spanish of all Spanish towns. The boastful native couplet which declares that —

> "Quien no ha visto a Sevilla,
> No ha visto a maravilla,"

is true enough, and if a traveler could only see one city in Spain he would do well to select the gay,

'A STREET IN SEVILLE.

growing, and thriving Seville in preference to all the rest. The streets are very narrow and crooked, and the houses are all either whitewashed or painted a very light pink, blue, or green shade, which contributes

not a little to the intolerable glare. In some of the
streets awnings are suspended from roof to roof, so
that you may drive under a canopy for some little
distance protected from the sun's rays. The houses
have patios, or interior courts, surrounded by balconies,
and in the dwellings of the rich these are very beautiful, being paved with marble tiles and ornamented
by tropical trees and plants, fountains, and flowers.
The open-work iron gates leading from the street to
the patios permit the passer-by to obtain charming
glimpses of these refreshing spots. Having rested all
day, we went out after nightfall, and viewed the place
by lamplight, with José for our guide. The principal
street is a crooked way about twenty feet wide, lined
with brilliantly lighted cafés and clubs, stores, places
of amusement, tavernas, etc., and thronged with
people. The big Plaza Nueva, to which reference has
been made, is also thronged with a constantly moving
crowd, lingering till long after midnight, affording an
unequaled opportunity to study the population in one
of its most characteristic aspects. There is not half as
much chattering and chaffing as would be observed in
a French crowd of the same dimensions; every one is
talking, but in a staid and reserved fashion, and it is
rare to hear an outburst of laughter. The shrill cry of
the aguadores, "Quien quiere agua?" is heard on
every hand, and they drive a brisk trade. The bands
play some strange Castilian airs, unlike anything you
have ever heard before, while you wait in vain to hear

a familiar strain from " Carmen " or " Il Barbiere,"
which would seem so appropriate to the time and
place. On this square is the *ayuntamiento*, or city hall,
beyond which is the old Plaza de la Constitucion, an
oblong square of such a quaint
aspect that one is inclined to
laugh when first its tumble-
down houses, with their innumerable crooked balconies,
meet the eye. Of course we
take a carriage-ride over the
Cristina, the great park-drive
by the edge of the Guadalquivir, where the
belles and beaux of
the town show them-
selves between seven
and eight o'clock in
their prettiest toilets.
The Cristina is the
finest promenade in
Spain and the place of
all places to see hand-
some women. The
Andalusians have some justification for their boasts
regarding the beauty and grace of their women ; the
average is certainly high. "There may be in England,
in France, or in Italy," says Gautier, "women of a more
perfect, more regular beauty, but assuredly there are

none prettier nor more *piquantes.*" They have in a
high degree what the Spaniards call *la sal:* not at all
like what is meant by Gallic salt, but something pecu-
liarly Andalusian and unique, — a mixture of dash,
piquancy, "savey," and deviltry. To say of an Andalusian maiden that she is salted, is regarded as the
highest possible compliment. We bring our strange
nocturnal round of sights to a close very late, after
visiting one of the subterranean cafés where gypsies
dance, and where we each drink a thimbleful of agua-
ardiente. It is impossible to describe the dancing
satisfactorily: not that it was indecent, for, on the
contrary, it was uncommonly decorous, but it was so
odd that it almost defies description. A troupe of four
men and four women occupied the stage. The females
were distinguished by the most extraordinarily bright
black eyes in the world, while they were otherwise not
by any means plain in appearance, though dressed
rather simply. The only music was a weird chant of a
peculiar and teasing rhythm, loud and shrill, accompanied by the regular clapping of hands; the same
motif ran through the whole, and all the company,
except the one who happened to be dancing, joined in
it with great gusto. The dancer began by stamping
with one and the other foot at irregular intervals, and
finally writhed from head to foot, waving the arms
meantime in a graceful fashion. Finally the middle
and upper portions of the body were brought into play,
and the most absurd and extravagant contortions of

the least graceful part of the system were produced.
This description will convey but a very inadequate idea
of the dance to any one except him who has seen it.
Nothing more thoroughly barbaric, more fantastic,

could be imagined in a dream. It was a *bolero*. In
having seen it we felt ourselves to be more fortunate
than M. Gautier, who erroneously assures his readers
that Spanish dances exist only in Paris, like those
shells which are found in curiosity-shops, but never on
the sea-beach.

The cathedral of Seville is so great a building in
many respects, that it is surely a surprise and a marvel
to the visitor who enters it with even the most ex-
aggerated anticipations. It is second to St. Peter's
alone in point of size, being 150 feet high, and 414
by 271 feet in dimensions inside, with 93 windows,

30 chapels, and everything in like proportions. Gautier says that Notre Dame of Paris might walk right up into the middle nave. "Pillars big as towers, and which appear frightfully frail, spring from the earth or hang from the vaulted roof like stalactites in a giant's cave. The four lateral naves, though less lofty, might shelter whole churches, spires and all. The retablo, or high altar, with its staircases, its superpositions of architecture, its rows on rows of statues, is an immense edifice of itself; it rises almost to the roof. The font-candle, large as a vessel's mast, weighs 2,050 pounds. Twenty thousand pounds of wax and as much oil are burned each year in the cathedral; the wine used in the holy sacrifice amounts to the frightful quantity of 18,750 litres. It is a fact that 500 masses are performed every day at the 80 altars. The catafalque used during Holy Week is nearly 100 feet high. The organs, of gigantic proportions, look like the basaltic colonnades of Fingal's Cave, and yet the storms and thunders that burst from their pipes, big as siege-guns, seem melodious murmurs, the distant songs of birds and seraphim, under these colossal arches." The cathedral staff consists of an archbishop and about one hundred priests. The chapter was immensely rich until the government appropriated its estates in 1836. The effect of the interior of the cathedral is majestic and solemn in the extreme, and the innumerable treasures of art, which it would take months to see and volumes to catalogue, are almost forgotten

in contemplating the superb vista of the nave.   But
the Spanish churches are always full of little artistic
museums abounding in pleasant surprises, and it will
never do to omit visiting this and that chapel, though
the process be never so wearisome. The details of the
interior in this case are worthy of the magnificent
edifice itself, which was designed to impress later generations with the belief that its builders were crazy.
The royal chapter contains the tombs of Alonso the
Wise and Queen Beatrix, St. Ferdinand, and Maria de
Padilla, the mistress of Pedro the Cruel. St. Ferdinand's body lies in a solid silver sarcophagus of beautiful workmanship, in front of the altar, the frontal of
which is also of silver. His sword, and the ivory
statuette of the Virgin which he carried about with him
in his campaigns, are here, with some other relics of
more than ordinary interest; and lastly, a portrait of
the conqueror of Seville, by Murillo. Of the most
interesting pictorial works of art in the cathedral,
I shall speak in another chapter.

The Giralda tower, built by the Moors about seven
hundred years ago, serves as bell-tower for the cathedral. So well built is the inclined plane up which the
Arabs rode their horses to the platform at the top,
some two hundred and fifty feet from the ground, that
it is just as strong to-day as the first day it was built.
The view of the city from the tower is very fine, but
the glare is awful. Yonder is the Alcazar, the ancient
palace of the Moorish monarchs; the tobacco-factory;

the palace of San Telmo, home of the Duke de Mont-pensier; the Tower of Gold, where the Moors used to store their valuables; the bull-ring, one of the best in Spain; and the winding Guadalquivir, gay with ship-ping, for the commerce of Seville is extensive. As this was the first river with any water in it we had seen in Spain, the sight of it glad-dened our eyes. A country as destitute of rivers, trees, and grass as is Spain is to be pitied.

It is wise to visit the Alcazar of Seville before seeing the Alhambra, for obvious reasons. The former was indeed the first Moorish building we saw, and consequently it impressed us strongly, all the more so that the repairs and restorations have made it present almost the same appearance that it wore in the time of Abdu-r-rahman Anna 'ssir Liddin-Allah. The King was intending to come here for a short sojourn at the time when his first wife, Mercedes, died; and about a dozen apartments had already been partly furnished for the occasion. The luxurious divans and tapestries presented to Alfonso by the last Sultan of

Turkey adorned several of the rooms. The Alcazar
is the only Moorish monument in Spain which has
been repainted, and, although a vast sum was expended
under Isabel, the moderns were not able to match the
blue tints of the Moors, which still excel all pigments
known to the Spaniards of to-day. The court of the
Doncellas, with its fifty white marble columns and its
walls covered with arabesques of indescribable delicacy
and intricacy, and the hall of ambassadors (the original
doors of which remain, untouched by the vandal hands
of Charles V, who had a mania for "improving" the
Moorish architecture, and did his best to spoil the
Alhambra), are the most remarkable portions of the
palace, which retains its Moorish character to a wonderful degree, considering how many Christians have
tampered with it since Sakkáf surrendered the city to
St. Ferdinand. The garden, with its terraces, bowers,
fountains, summer-houses, banana-trees, orange-trees,
lemon-trees, pomegranates, date-palms (all bearing
fruit), jasmins, magnolias, citrons, prickly-pears, and
so forth, seemed almost too beautiful to be real; but
there was much reality in the overpowering rays of the
fierce sun which occasionally beat upon our heads
while we wandered in its labyrinth and inhaled the
scent of the orange-blossoms with which the air was
laden—and dodged the bees. Here is the pond
where Philip V used to fish, and the Moorish baths
where the beauties of the harem disported themselves long before; and now and then the visitor steps

on the wrong paving-stone in the pathway and is sprinkled by a fine jet of spray from an unseen fountain. The luxurious Moors had a covered gallery running all along one side of the garden, so they could walk out without exposure to the sun. The thing that pleased us most was to see great bunches of bananas growing on the trees. It was hard to realize that this superb palace was uninhabited; but that is the case with a great many royal palaces in these days of republics and iconoclasm.

The tobacco-factory is one of the most interesting things to be seen in Seville. Seven thousand five hundred women and girls are employed. The building is immense, the dimensions being 662 by 524 feet. It was very uncomfortably hot, and in some of the rooms the odor of tobacco was exceedingly strong, but José said that the work was wholesome, that once when a plague devastated the city not a single *cigarrera* was sick, and he added that vermin gave the establishment and the employees a wide berth. The girls were very decidedly *décolletées*, and some of them came startlingly near to wearing nothing at all, but they usually threw a light shawl over their shoulders when they saw a party of male visitors approaching. One room alone contained no less than 3,300 women. As we entered, the sound of their voices was like the distant roar of the breakers on an ocean strand. The cigarreras, many of whom are great beauties, form a class by themselves, and unhappily are not noted for their chastity. Of course we thought of the "Carmen" of the opera, and on coming out of the factory were pleased to discover that the infantry barracks occupied the opposite side of the square, thus verifying the first scene of Bizet's work. This is not the only pleasant association connected with Seville; for, besides the world-renowned Figaro, another true Andalusian type, there is Don Juan, who lived in a house now belonging to the nuns of San Leandro. It is interesting to compare the numerous contradictory legends about this immortal gay deceiver. The most universally accepted story makes his name Don Juan Tenorio, and was first given to the

world by Gabriel Tellez (Tirso de Molina). Then after serving as the hero of various Italian and French plays, he was finally immortalized in the book of Mozart's opera. The original of Donna Anna was the daughter of the Governor of Seville, whom Don Juan killed, and whose statue so unexpectedly (and, I may add, so operatically) accepted a foolish invitation to supper, thus affording another proof, if one were needed, that the Spaniards do not always need to be urged to accept the courtesies offered them! Indeed the statue not only accepted Don Juan's invitation at once, but when he invited him to supper in return Don Juan was equally ready to accept the hospitalities of the statue. But the most picturesque legend told in Seville makes it appear that Don Juan lived to repent of his evil deeds, and founded the hospital now

known as the Charity. The story runs, that, going home one night after an orgie, Don Juan met a funeral procession going to the church of St. Isidore — black-robed, masked monks, bearing yellow wax tapers, something more dreadful indeed than an ordinary funeral. "Who is dead?" asked Don Juan: "a husband killed in a duel by his wife's lover? or an honest father who was too slow about leaving his fortune to his heirs?" One of the bearers of the bier answered: "This dead man is none other than Don Juan de

Marana, whose obsequies we are about to perform.
Come with us and pray for him." Don Juan
approached and, by the light of the candles, perceived
that the corpse had his face, and in fact was himself.
He followed his own bier into the church and prayed
with the mysterious monks : the following morning he
was found lying, unconscious, on the steps of the
choir. This incident made such an impression on
him that he renounced his depraved way of life,
became a penitent, and, after founding the aforesaid
hospital, died almost in the odor of sanctity.

CHAPTER X.

PICTURES IN SEVILLE.

SOME of the most interesting of Murillo's works are still retained in his own city, though the French under Soult carried off a good many valuable examples, including the large Conception, in the Louvre, and the St. Elizabeth which has found its way back as far as Madrid. "The Vision of Saint Anthony of Padua," which hangs in the chapel of the baptistry of the cathedral, is a great painting in all respects,* and is

---

* "Jamais la magie de la peinture n'a été poussée plus loin," says Gautier, in a burst of admiration. " Le saint en extase est à genoux au milieu de la cellule, dont tous les pauvres détails sont rendus avec cette réalité vigoureuse qui caractérise l'école espagnole. A travers la porte entr'ouverte l'on aperçoit un de ces longs cloîtres blancs en arcades si favorables à la rêverie. Le haut du tableau noyé d'une lumière blonde, transparente, vaporeuse, est occupé par des groupes d'anges d'une beauté vraiment idéale. Attiré par la force de la prière, l'Enfant Jésus descend de nuée en nuée et va se placer entre les bras du saint personnage, dont la tête est baignée d'effluves rayonnantes et se renverse dans un spasme de volupté céleste. Je mets ce tableau divin au-dessus de la Sainte Elisabeth de Hongrie pansant un teigneux que l'on voit à l'Académie de Madrid, au-dessus de Moïse, au-dessus de toutes les Vierges et des enfants du maître, si beaux et si purs qu'ils soient. Qui n'a pas vu le Saint Antoine de Padoue ne connaît pas le dernier mot du peintre de Séville ; c'est comme ceux qui s'imaginent connaître Rubens et qui n'ont pas vu la Madeleine d'Anvers."

considered by some writers to be the finest of Murillo's
works. It has extraordinary gusto, and the motive
must appeal forcibly to every observer, in spite of the
absence of the feminine element which constitutes such
an important factor in many of this painter's most
admirable pictures.   There is a charming tenderness
and benignity about the Saint's expression, and I may
say that no painter, as it seems to me, has represented
so truthfully and graciously the softer side of men's
character — that phase of feeling which all have
experienced at some crisis in life, but which most men
(especially those of Northern race) are ashamed of.
Murillo's art must impress Protestants and sceptics
with the sincerity and depth of his faith, its beneficent
influence upon him, and its value as an art motive.
His religious fervor supplies him with an inspiration
which lifts his art to a plane where simplicity, grandeur,
and dignity become the natural concomitants of a lofty
ideal.   Where the modern man expends his emotional
reserves in his family affections, the Catholic pours out
all his love and reverence before the altar of the
Virgin and her Divine Son. In the face of Saint
Anthony, as here depicted, there is the same deep and
tranquil joy that may be seen in a father's face when
he welcomes a child who has been absent. " Drawn
by the force of prayer," — that is very fine, very touching, but not more so than the daily miracles of human
love which are perhaps quite as authentic.   This
painting has a history not wholly unconnected with

that New World which Columbus so prematurely
presented to Castile and Léon. One morning at an
early hour a man enveloped in a long cloak entered
the cathedral, apparently for the purposes of worship,
and turned into the chapel of the baptistry, where —
as soon as he perceived that he was alone and unob-
served — he slipped out a knife from his belt and
quickly cut the lower part of the canvas out of the
frame ; then he rolled up the stolen masterpiece and
concealing it under his cloak, made good his escape.
As soon as the theft became known, the government
advertised it far and wide, sending out descriptions of
the painting. The thief brought his booty to America,
and one day offered to sell it to a picture-dealer in
New York, but of course the latter had heard of the
theft and promptly notified the Spanish Consul, so
that the missing painting was finally found, sent back
to Seville, and restored to its old place, the work of
joining it to the other parts of the canvas being so
skilfully done that it is not easy to tell where the
patching was done. As for the foolish thief, he was
caught, to be sure, but at that time he could not be
punished, owing to the want of an extradition treaty
between the United States and Spain.

The cathedral is very rich in works of art by painters
of the Sevillian school, — Herrera, Cano, Campaña,
Valdès, Vargas, and others. There is an exquisite
"Guardian Angel," by Murillo, and in the sacristy,
where the great " painter of the Conceptions " lies

buried, are two fine canvases by him, "San Isidro" and
" San Leandro." The altarpiece, a " Descent from the
Cross," by Campaña, was greatly admired by Murillo,
who was buried here at his own request, just in front
of it. Among other paintings is one of the patron
saints of Seville, Saints Justa and Rufina. There are
two different tales about the models who posed for this
work ; but the favorite version is to the effect that they
were two frail ladies of Madrid — frail morally, I mean.
Another chapel contains no less than nine pictures by
Zurbarán, but I will not mention any more of the cathedral's artistic treasures, for I do not wish to poach on
the preserves of the guidebook-makers, wretchedly as
they have done their work.

The Charity Hospital contains Murillo's " Moses
Striking the Rock " and the " Miracle of the Loaves
and Fishes." I translate the following agreeable
description of a celebrated canvas by Valdès Leal in
the same place : A dead archbishop is seen lying in
a rotten coffin trimmed with velvet. On one of the
fingers of his gloved hand shines an enormous ring.
The greenish, bluish, black head is in a complete state
of putrefaction under the white mitre surrounded by
pearls. Viscid larvæ crawl over the gnawed nose ; an
unclean creature emerges from one of the eyes. At
the side of the archbishop, in another coffin, a king,
with a crown upon his head, is laid out under a swarm
of worms. The clenched hand grasps a sceptre.
Above, through the clouds, appears a hand holding

a pair of scales, and against a luminous ray of light flame the words of truth : " Here below, all is vanity." *

The property of the Academy of Fine Arts is lodged in an old church, ill-lighted, but high and airy, and it is called the Provincial Museum. It contains twenty-four pictures by Murillo, twenty by Zurbarán, nineteen by Pacheco, twelve by the brothers Polancos, ten by the elder Herrera, ten by Valdès Leal, and the rest are by Juan del Castillo, Andrès Perez, Juan Simon Gutierrez, Francisco Frutet, Pablo de Céspedes, Matías Arteaga y Alfaro, Estéban Marquez, Juan de las Roelas, Clemente Torres, Francisco Varela, Alonso Vazquez, and other gentlemen of equally sonorous names, belonging to the three epochs in art to which everything in Seville is relegated, namely : the ante-Murillo epoch, the Murillo epoch, and the post-Murillo epoch. The whole collection numbers less than two hundred pictures. Many of them are in a very dirty and obscured condition, and a large number are of slight interest to the casual visitor, though they supply much food for reflection to the student of art. The " Saint Thomas Aquinas," of Zurbarán, is of capital importance, ranking first among this prominent painter's performances.† There is a certain academic dryness and

---

* " Ici-bas, rien n'est vrai." P. L. Imbert, " L'Espagne: Splendeurs et Misères."

† This is the description of the work given by the catalogue: " Representa el Santo en pié y elevado: en la parte superior, y entre nubes, se ven Jesucristo y la Vírgen, San Pablo y Santo Domingo: á los lados del Santo aparecen sentados, tambien sobre nubes, los cuatro Doctores de la Iglesia Latina: y abajo, en primer término, están arrodillados el Emperador Cárlos V, el Arzobispo de Deza y algunos otros personajes. Es tradicional que la cabeza que se ve inmediatamente detrás del Emperador es el retrato de su autor."

formality in his works generally, and this unpleasant
quality pervades many of the paintings of the Sevillian
school in this gallery, — paintings of wooden saints,
stupid monks, lifeless apostles, and automatic angels,
which are libels upon humanity and outrages against
divinity. It is only when you turn to Murillo that you
find vitality and thought in form and color. See with
what legible expression and individuality he has
endowed his benign " San Antonio," the good-hearted
and tender man who holds the Niño Dios in his arms
so lovingly! And note the Virgin Mother of " La Ser-
villeta," so full of holy maternal affection and solicitude,
" admiracion de cuantos la ven," as the catalogue
quaintly says. It is not hard to see what places the
master so far above the rest of them who went before
and after him, for if it may be said of many that they
could draw to perfection, of others that they were
superb in point of coloring, of a few men that their
knowledge of *chiaroscuro* was great, of how many can
it be said as well that they combined these acquire-
ments with the perceptions of a genuine artist, the
enthusiasms of a noble and sincere man, and the
sensitive nature of a poet? Happy Murillo! and
fortunate Spain! to possess such glorious memorials
of this "divinely gifted man." Can it be possible that
this very Seville which was his home was also the
scene of the Inquisition? and that the same religion
which prompted his labors was capable of inspiring
the fiendish tortures by which Torquemada cast an
ineffaceable stain upon his church and his country?

CHAPTER XI.

SEVILLE TO GRANADA.

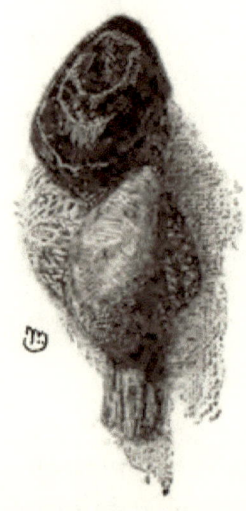

To the fevered traveler in hot Seville there comes a vision of Granada with her breezy hills and her distant snow-capped sierras! We reluctantly gave up going to Cadiz and Gibraltar, and told José we would fain hie us to the Alhambra. He asked us to what hôtel we were going, and we responded, as in duty bound, "The Washington Irving." "The Hôtel of the Seven Floors is better," said José. "We will go there, then," we said: "for there are degrees of badness, and some bad dishes are not so hopelessly bad as others." José packed a lunch consisting of cold meats, bread, fruit, and a bottle of Manzanilla, in a basket, and we took it with us, for it was more than doubtful whether we were to be victualled at Utrera, or at La Roda, or at Bobadilla, though we knew that the "through car" which leaves Seville daily at seven A. M., and arrives at Granada about fourteen hours later, was to be switched from one line to another at each of those three interesting junctions. José came to the station to say " Hasta la vista " to us, and we departed, leaving him richer by a handful of pesetas, for truly the worthy fellow had been of great service to us, missing at least two siestas in our behalf, and had assisted Hermano to select a black lace toca for his far-off *muchacha* with good taste and judgment, — without pocketing more than ten or twelve pesetas as a commission, which was modest and reasonable.

That was a day which may without exaggeration be set down as warm.   At Utrera our car was left behind by the train, which proceeded to Cadiz, and after an hour and a half of waiting we were picked up by another train and moved eastward at the usual rate of sixteen miles an hour till we came to La Roda, on the line between Cordova and Malaga.   Here we spent a pleasant hour on a siding, and presently the south-ward train took us along as far as Bobadilla, and there dropped us.   There was a restaurant at Bobadilla, but we had no time to spare, for the final stage of this extraordinary journey was at once entered upon, and we were at last fairly on the Granada road.   The latter part of the ride is most interesting, and our anticipa-tions are excited to the highest degree.   At nightfall we are toiling up a steep grade among the romantic and oddly picturesque mountain defiles, where gray villages, perched on gray, rocky hillsides, overlook the grim gray landscape beneath, and where ruined castles and citadels loom up suddenly in the twilight on the barren mountain slopes, as unreal and mysterious as the castles in Spain of our waking dreams! This is the most lonesome, ghostly region in Spain. The mountains are of peculiar forms, and their ruddy flanks look as if some Titanic colorists had given them a coat of Indian red, here and there covered with a gray glaze. We have passed Antequera, Archidona, and Loja. Each name awakens recollections of Irving's "Conquest of Granada." It was among these strange mountains that Ferdinand and his warlike spouse gave and took so many sturdy blows in the long conflict which Fray Antonio Agapida has recorded with so much romantic zest. If one could travel among the mountains on the moon, they would be found not unlike these ashen-hued and ghostly heights, which show one how a dead world might appear. Is it possible that the rest of the physical world can be as venerable as this part of it? The sun has fairly gone down when the train reaches the open plain which encircles Granada.

> "Yet of the Vega not a rood
> But hath been drenched with Moorish blood."

Proceeding from the Loja station, the scene of old
Ali Atar's bloody chastisement upon the Christian army
which had marched down from Cordova so proudly,
we are just in time to catch one glimpse of the distant
snows of the Sierra Nevada, " with rosy stain " now
fading fast. It is our entrance upon the vast arena
called the Vega, or plain, and across which in the
gathering shadows of the evening the train rolls slowly
until the Granada station is reached. The coach which
conveys the weary traveler to the Hôtel of the Seven
Floors is drawn by four gaunt mules, which look as
if they lived on shavings, but who are in recompense
decorated profusely with gaudy red tassels. The
town, or at least a large portion of it, is traversed, the
bull-ring being passed soon after quitting the railway
station.   Presently we are climbing through a thick
grove, and our hearts beat quicker to know that we
are on the hill where stands the Alhambra.   It is
pitch-dark, and nothing can be seen under the trees,
but there is a delicious sound of gurgling, rushing
water, for on all sides are little rills dashing down the
steep slopes.   A few minutes later, we are in the
hôtel, ordering a supper in three or four languages,
and reading a bundle of letters from home.

CHAPTER XII.

THE SEVEN FLOORS.

"SEÑORITO, un cuartito!"

"Monsieur, un sou, un petit sou!"

"Mister! a penny!"

Those dirty four-year-old girls had learned to beg in three languages. But they were picturesque in their rags, or, as Hermano said, they were merely a part of the general picturesqueness all about us. When they found that we were unmoved by their appeals, one of them planted herself squarely in front of us (we were sitting on a stone bench overlooking the town and the Vega) and began to dance the bolero in the most business-like manner. After we had got rid of these juvenile beggars, Hermano produced from his pocket a card from which he proceeded to read the following list of "curiosities of the city of Granada and its environs," or "curiosidades de la ciudad de Granada y sus

cercanias": Alhambra, Axarix, Audiencia, Algibe de
la lluvia, Albercon de los Negros, Albaicin, Baños de
las Damas, Baños Arabes, Catedral, Capilla Real,
Cartuja, Casa de los Tiros, Espada de Boabdil, Ermita
de San Sebastian, Fuente de Alfacar, Fuente del Avel-
lano, S. Gerónimo (Sepulcro del Gran Capitan), Sierra
Nevada, Suspiro del Moro, Sacro-Monte, Soto de
Roma, Palacio de Andaralik, Palacio de Aben-Abid,
Palacio de Viznar.

"And here we have been spending nearly twenty-
four hours in this place without doing a thing, unless
it is to make José Gadea understand that that *ropa*

must be washed and ironed
by next *Martes tardes*," I
said. (I was growing very
proud of the Spanish phrases
I had picked up.)

"Yes," assented Hermano,
glancing over the list of curiosities, which seemed to exercise a certain painful fascination upon him. "Do you
suppose they would admit
us to see the *Baños de las
damas?*"

"Nicolás could tell you."
Nicolás Garzon Rodriguez
had not yet made his appearance that morning, though
it was quite late. He was a cross-eyed youth, who

spoke a few words of French and fewer still of English, and we had engaged him to be our guide for a day or two, until we had got our bearings. Nicolás was an amusing fellow. He was smoking cigarettes continually, except when eating, sleeping, or in church. He was entirely willing to accompany us anywhere all the morning, but wisely insisted on taking his regular siesta after the noonday meal, in which respect we followed his excellent example, and indeed continued the practice until we left the country. He insisted that the Arabic inscription, — "Wa la gháliba illa Alláh" ("There is no conqueror but God"), Alhamar's motto, — repeated here and there on the walls of the Alhambra, meant "Good-ah God." He remarked also that he could tell an Englishman from an American, because the former said "Red towers," the latter "Vermilion towers." He held that the chief point of interest about the Generalife was the gardener's daughter, who, like the miller's daughter, is grown "so dear, so dear," that it costs four reales to have her mother show you through the garden, in order to have a look at the maiden's prettiness as you pass the porter's lodge. There were other entertaining traits about Nicolás, who was quite dignified in demeanor, but whose heart we won by treating him to bottled beer and Cuban cigars in the garden of the hôtel. Travelers assuredly make a great mistake when they do not cultivate the acquaintance of their guides. To us Nicolás was quite as interesting as the Alhambra, over

which he possessed one decided advantage, namely:
that we had never heard of him before.

The Hôtel of the Seven Floors is just outside the
walls of the Moorish fortress, and takes its name from
the Tower of the Seven Floors, which stands in the
rear of the house and which has an entertaining
legend, one of the best that Irving tells, concerning
the Moor's legacy of treasure which enriched poor
Pedro Gil, the water-carrier. Opposite this house is
the Hôtel Washington Irving, which, though older
and perhaps more widely known, is not so popular as
its rival. These two are the only hôtels on the hill.
They are situated on a spot not only beautiful in its
natural aspects, but exceedingly romantic from its
associations. The landlord of the Seven Floors is a fat
and jolly old boy, and his daughter is remarkably
pretty — two circumstances which may in some

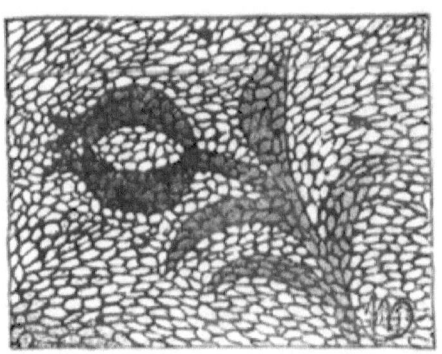

measure account for the
popularity of the inn.
The sociable group of
boarders, which gath-
ered just outside the
front door on the in-
geniously designed
pavement of black and
white pebbles, was often
enlivened in the afternoon and evening by the presence
and animated conversation of this dark-eyed belle, who
slept on a bench in the "office" when the hôtel was

crowded; at least we saw her slumbering there at three o'clock in the morning on the day when we departed by an early train.

The visitors' book in the public room was full of enthusiastic praise of the accommodations, cuisine, service, etc., these absurd testimonials being written in Spanish, French, English, and German, with an occasional impromptu verse or a labored joke. One Englishman had filled a whole page with an " Ode to Carlos Quinto," which was really witty. The fare at this place was very bad, though probably it would be rated a good example of a high-class table, as Spanish tables go. It was diverting to see a beautiful woman at dinner, eating cold fish in oil with her knife. She looked like Marie Roze, or would have looked like her if she had not been cross-eyed, as so many Spanish beauties are. *Mesa redonda* (*table d'hôte*) was served in the long dining-room at six o'clock, when it happened to be ready on time, which was a rare occurrence. But most of the visitors preferred to take dinner in the picturesque terraced garden, under the shadow of the Alhambra walls, where the lamps were lit and cigarettes glowed in the dusk. Here the only drawback to the enjoyment of dining *al fresco* — a privilege so wisely esteemed by Europeans — was the presence of several half-starved cats, who, when one's attention strayed from the edibles to some less important subject, impudently jumped upon the tables, and seizing whatever food they could most conven-

iently reach, made off with it rapidly and in triumph.
One evening, as we sat here at dinner, a party of
toreros came up from the town, and created a tremendous excitement which quite paralyzed for the time
being the usefulness of the waiters, who hung about
the demi-gods of the arena in an ecstacy of admiration.
The dinner that evening was neglected, and the entire
establishment was thrown into a commotion. It was in
this pretty garden that we met the only compatriots we
had encountered in Spain — Mr. L., the author, and
Mr. R., the artist. It was surprising to find how
pessimistic our group could be under such pleasant
circumstances. Instead of rhapsodizing about castles,
cathedrals, and pictures, the quartet unanimously fell
to complaining of the heat, anathematizing the beggars,
abusing the hôtels and railways, and outdoing one
another in preposterous stories about fleas. Mr. R.
was in a particularly gloomy state of mind. He had
been made downright ill by the smells of Burgos; at
Toledo he had been obliged to go out in the street to
look up the hôtel employees and inform them that it
was past dinner-time; and he was sighing for beloved
France, where he could make himself understood.
While we were talking, some strolling *caballero* in the
grove near by struck up the familiar, wild, ear-piercing
chant which apparently forms the sole stock-in-trade
of Spanish vocalists, and as the last mournful howl
died away in the distance, a groan broke from the
afflicted artist, and he said, " I am so tired of that

song!" But we on our part had a special personal grievance which made his woes seem trifles light as air. Our bedchambers were immediately above the donkeys' stables! And those frisky animals spent the greater part of each night in kicking against the walls of their quarters with tremendous vigor, occasionally breaking out into a prolonged and startling he-haw of fiendish fury. When we told Mr. R. of these things he acknowledged that his cup was not yet so full as it might be.

CHAPTER XIII.

Do you remember what Daisy Miller's mother said soon after her arrival in Rome? " We had heard so much about it; I suppose we had heard too much. But we couldn't help that. We had been led to expect something different." Likewise do you remember what Edward Everett Hale's double used to say when called upon for a speech? " So much has been said, and so well, that I will not occupy the time."

No one can adequately describe the Alhambra: not even Irving, whose word-pictures are so beautiful and so full of the local color. He comes nearest to it, and we felt a certain patriotic pride as we entered the place and remembered that an American had sat upon the throne of Boabdil to such good purpose. On the first visit there is a feeling of disappointment, for the imaginary Alhambra which has been built in the mind by means of reading has to be demolished, — a painful and shocking process, which is soon over. Nicolás led us about, told us what to admire, catalogued the courts and halls, and conducted us to the towers. We went back to the hôtel disgusted. But the next day we gave Nicolás the slip, and went in the right way to enjoy ourselves — alone, aimless, lazy, and in sympathy with the place. That long, quiet, peaceful, beautiful afternoon spent in the Hall of Ambassadors will be forever remembered. We sat in a window overlooking the valley of the Darro, and for hours we did not care to move or speak. "While the city below pants with the noontide heat," says Irving, in one of his most exquisite passages of description, "and the parched Vega trembles to the eye, the delicate airs from the Sierra Nevada play through these lofty halls, bringing with them the sweetness of the surrounding gardens. Everything invites to that indolent repose, the bliss of Southern climes; and while the half-shut eye looks out from shaded balconies upon the glittering landscape, the ear is lulled by the rustling of groves and the murmur of running streams."

At another time we loitered long in the charming
boudoir of Lindaraxa, where we amused ourselves by
making sketches of the opposite wing, the *tocador de
la Reyna*, where Irving lodged. The little garden is
overgrown with orange and citron trees, vines, and
rank growths unknown to Northern countries, and it
has a melancholy air of having seen better days.
Then, wandering slowly from one hall to another, as
the magic hour of sunset drew near, we would go to
the charming garden on the battlemented wall under
the bell-tower, looking off on the Vega, the wide-
spreading city below us, the Vermilion Towers on the
thickly wooded hillside, and the

> " Mountain walls that bound
> The glorious landscape spread around,
> Which, canopied by cloudless skies,
> A scene of matchless beauty lies."

To convey an idea of the spirit of such a scene
would be a task to call forth all the powers of a poet.
Such episodes as these remain a source of inexhaustible pleasure for years ; you have but to close your
eyes and you may see it all again, long after your
discriminating memory has cast out all the disagreeable
things. The strangeness of that marvelous combination
— Roman towers, groves, the great town beneath with
its vesper bells sounding through the still evening air,
the vast plain and the gigantic snow-peaks — is not
less impressive than its beauty. No wonder that poets

and painters celebrate this wonderful corner of the
world! In the twilight, on a ruined tower's platform,
it is easy to forget petty griefs, and to believe that life
contains more of beauty than of ugliness.

The subtle influences of the place and time so
affected Hermano that he improvised the following
legend of the Vermilion Towers : —

"Long before the days of His Whitewashing
Majesty Carlos Quinto, when tourists were unknown
and Christians were at a discount in this region, the
eminent and highly esteemed Abou Mansard came
over here from Morocco, where he had made a fortune
in the manufacture of a well-known brand of prayer-
rugs, and bought the towers yonder (then known as
the old Phœnician grain-elevators), for the purpose
of making his summer home there. He brought his
wives with him, and his daughters, among them the
lovely and fascinating Tortilla, who wore red slippers
turned up at the toes, not over two inches long, and,
among other clothes, a brass necklace which was considered very nobby. Same as you see on the Rue de
Rivoli, don't you know? Ab. went to work and fitted
up his towers regardless of expense. He had that
odd-looking terrace, which has dungeons under it,
thrown out on the right, to afford an open-air promenade for the women, and he introduced all the ancient
improvements — fountains, arabesques, tiles, grotto-
work, till you couldn't rest. He became quite
influential in the Alhambra, and was regarded as one

of the solid men. One day he bagged a young
Christian Knight down towards Antequera in a
skirmish, and brought him home as a captive, placing
him in one of the best dungeons. The name of the
unfortunate Spaniard was Don Miguel Dulce Cabello
de Angel, and he was a *Christiano viejo* from 'way
back, with a pedigree as long as your arm, and

a brilliant pair of black eyes and an arched instep.
It would make you wild with envy to see him roll
a cigarette, and for graceful and daring horsemanship
he took the cake. Tortilla was walking on the terrace
one evening when she heard the young prisoner
singing in a mellow tenor voice a Castilian ditty; it
was thus he whiled away the weary hours in his lonely
cell. The sound seemed to proceed from beneath her
very feet, and her susceptible nature was stirred to its

depths, for she had never before heard the soulful
strains of 'Little Buttercup' and 'The Last Rose of
Summer.' She ran to the parapet with a tumultuously
throbbing heart, and leaned over as far as she could,
but all she could make out in the dusk was a small
window, about the size of a porthole, in the wall about
six feet below the top. The sounds of music now
appeared to her to come from that window, and they
were sadder than ever, for Don Miguel was feeling
all broken up, and had begun to sing 'Put Me in My
Little Bed.' As soon as he had finished, Tortilla gave
a little cough.

" ' Ahem ! '

" It was heard. In a moment the noble Don's head
was thrust out of the window, — but he was looking
down into the grove below.

" 'Ahem !' repeated Tortilla.

" He looked up, and said, with sudden admiration :
' What a daisy ! '

" Tortilla could not comprehend this Christian
compliment, but she blushed, and asked the gentleman
what was his name and how he came to be so miserably
situated. When he had explained matters, she introduced herself in turn, and they continued their
conversation until Tortilla, saying she feared she would
be missed in the castle if she stayed longer, bade her
new acquaintance a sweet good-night, much to his
sorrow, and retired, leaving him in a thoroughly
agitated condition.

"'A mash!' he groaned, as he sank back upon his rude couch, torn with a perfect bull-fight of emotions, 'and here I am in durance vile, with no way of escape.'

"But Tortilla came again to the parapet, every evening when there was no one else on the terrace to see her, and they had many hours of affectionate converse. In the meantime old Ab. did not tumble to the racket.

One evening Tortilla said to Don Miguel:—

"'I have good news for you. They say that the Cid is coming with a big army of Christians, and that he has sworn to conquer Granada this time, if it takes a leg.'

"'Hooray!' cried Don Miguel.

"'But if my governor should kick the bucket in the fray, it would be a cold day for me,' said the Moorish maid, pensively.

"'Never mind, Tortilla *mia*, I will wed thee at once, and don't you forget it,' ejaculated the impulsive knight, throwing her a kiss.

"As she had announced, the Cid with his hosts was getting ready to go for 'em, and not long afterwards there was a red-hot combat down on the Vega. Don Miguel could not see the fun from his porthole, but he could hear the Spaniards shouting out their battle-song:—

> 'Debout! enfants de l'Iberie! ·
> Haut les glaives et haut les cœurs!
> Des paiens nous serons vainqueurs,
> Ou nous mourrons pour la patrie!'

" The battle was long and severe. About noon,
when victory seemed about to perch upon the standards
of the Moors, both sides retired to take their customary
siestas, after which they began again, and at the close
of a struggle of unequaled fierceness, the heathen were
beaten, having been outnumbered two to one. The
Cid, accompanied by Felipe Segundo, Carlos Quinto,
and others of his staff, took possession of the place.
Don Miguel regained his freedom, and taking the
blushing Tortilla by the hand, he led her into the
presence of the Cid, and announced that he would like
to espouse her.

" ' What are you giving us, Don Miguel ? ' said the
Cid, wrathfully; ' she is a heathen jade. Besides I
had picked her out for myself.'

" Without commenting upon the inconsistency of
the great warrior, Don Miguel contented himself
with remarking that the maiden had plighted her
troth to him, and that he would die sooner than give
her up!

" The Cid was a wily old chap, and had an extensive
knowledge of human nature. Turning to Tortilla, he
said: ' It must be for you to choose between us, my
dear. If you choose Don Miguel, I shall be under the
painful necessity of drinking his gore by the quart.
If you choose me, you will be rich and happy, besides
being the wife of the greatest fighter that ever lived ;
in fact, you will be the Cidess.'

" True to the treacherous and mercenary nature

of her sex, the false creature decided in favor of the Cid, and was married to him with great *éclat* at once.

"Don Miguel Dulce Cabello de Angel went to the highest platform of the highest tower, drew a razor from his pocket, and in the view of all the grandees

of Castile, Léon, Aragon, Catalonia, Navarre, La Mancha, Valencia, Murcia, Estremadura, Andalusia, the Asturias, Galicia, the Basque Provinces, and New Jersey, he spilled the richest, reddest, bluest blood in all Spain all over the towers, — hence the Vermilion Towers."

As Hermano concluded his legend, the towers at

which we were gazing assumed a more distinct and pronounced hue of color, as the last faint reflection from the ruddy Western skies lingered about their ancient battlements.

"See!" I said: "The towers are blushing on account of the lies told about them."

CHAPTER XIV.

Down in the city it was unspeakably hot, and we spent very little time there. Nicolás persuaded us that we ought to devote at least one day to the sights of the town, so we started early in the morning, and went first to the cathedral. This is a most repulsive structure, which inspired Hermano with a sudden and violent aversion for Catholicism. The numerous mean chapels are full of tawdry ecclesiastical bric-à-brac and impossible works of art. The old women kneeling in front of the altars got up from their prayers to beset us for alms, and followed us about until they got something. Nicolás carried about a lighted cigarette, which he perilously concealed in the pocket of his coat, enjoying a surreptitious whiff once in a while in an obscure chapel. The six enormous paintings, by Alonso Cano, which adorn the *capilla mayor* are in the most artificial and formal vein, and we

found it easy to believe that the author of such mon-
strous works was capable of murdering his wife : he
certainly had no feeling. To go from the Alhambra
down into such a dismal, whitewashed granite barrack
as this cathedral is enough to make a Christian wish
himself " a pagan suckled by a creed outworn." The
capilla real contains the mortal remains of the Catholic
sovereigns Ferdinand and Isabella. A richly sculptured
sarcophagus of marble, with recumbent alabaster effi-
gies of the pious conquerors of Granada, surmounts
the narrow vault where the leaden coffins are. We
did not go down there, but, among the many favorite
"gags" derived from Ford's highly amusing volume,
this struck us as especially funny ;   " Tomb of Ferdinand and Isabella. . . . Mind your head." The place
is impressive in spite of the cheap, theatrical accessories
and the junkshop atmosphere. One thinks of Prescott,
and, for the second time in Granada, feels a thrill of
patriotic pride.

   To go to the Carthusian monastery we took a carriage, and monopolized what room there was in the
streets, forcing pedestrians to skip into the doorways,
and several times causing a blockade of mules.
Nicolás was happy. This sort of thing just suited
him, and the cracking of the driver's whip seemed
to afford him the most unalloyed pleasure. As we
meandered through the crooked ways, past houses
decorated with all sorts of odd green, pink, and blue
designs, under little balconies half hid by coarse

curtains, he became communicative, and gossiped in a genial way about his life and adventures. There is no subject so interesting to a man as himself.

It was true, he said, that when you met ladies of your acquaintance at a restaurant or a café, it was proper to call the waiter to you and quickly pay their bill; this was one of the little points of etiquette about which we had entertained doubts. He gave us illustrations from his own experience and observation, and he scoffed at the suggestion that ladies might be apt to go to places where they would be certain to meet their male friends, — that is, they would not do so from mercenary motives, he added, with a wink. The Cartuja proved to be interesting, though the monks have all gone, and with them many works of art. The church and chapels contain a large amount and variety of fine marbles, carved with more or less artistic success. The arabesques in the church are of wonderful intricacy and abundance. At one end of a long bare hall, there is a cross, high up on the white wall, against which it stands out in relief. Nicolás asked us of what wood we thought the cross was made. When we had guessed, he took us up close enough to demonstrate that it was painted on the wall itself.

The Granada beggars are the most troublesome of all their tribe, and there are few places to which they do not penetrate. Nicolás introduced us to the gypsy quarter on the steep hill of the Albaycin, and

we entered a squalid cave-dwelling inhabited by a
blear-eyed brigand of a blacksmith, his excessively
dirty children, and a couple of black pigs, — " local
color ! " — for the purpose of seeing a couple of horrid
youngsters dance a bolero. When the performance
was about concluded, in a thoughtless moment
Hermano took a few coppers from his pocket and gave
them to the children. Presto ! in less time than it
takes to tell it, a score of hideous creatures swarmed
about us with frantic, vociferous appeals and threaten-
ing looks and gestures. They seemed to spring out
of the ground. We were taken by surprise, and it
cost us a pretty penny to get out of the place, for
of course it did no good under such circumstances
to repeat " Perdone Usted, por Dios, hermano ! " The
wretches chased us until Nicolás showed fight, and we
were soon out of their territory. This is the part
of Granada containing the most remains of Moorish
dwellings, and in several patios their light, delicate,
airy, and graceful architectural effects may be found,
in greater or less perfection. Here are the " bits "
that Fortuny alone could paint, — the vast expanse
of white wall, half in shadow and half in light, the
great arched portal giving access to the cool interior
with its slim pillars, its arabesques and tiles, its swing-
ing lamps, its inlaid doors, its fountains, alcoves,
alabaster pavement, and glimpses of embowered
gardens beyond. Nothing is wanting but the Moor
himself, as Fortuny represented him, sitting cross-

legged on his rug, contemplating space, and busily
thinking about nothing. Some one has said that
what Chopin is to music Fortuny is to art, and that
both of them "have more of the gypsy wildness and
strangeness of Spain in their works than of the sweet,
classical composure of Italy, or of the sharp, graceful
esprit of France."

The Generalife was a royal summer residence of
the Moors, and occupied a higher site than the Alhambra, on a hillside commanding a very extensive pros-
pect. All that is left of it, beyond a few bare apartments whose beautiful arabesques have been whitewashed, is the romantic garden, irrigated by countless
little brooks and fountains, and overgrown with a riot-
ous abundance of tropical plants, trees, and flowers.
Winding paths everywhere serve but to lose you in
a sweet-scented jungle of blooming shrubbery. The
bees bustle about with great energy, too much occupied to take note of human intruders; and the gurgling of unseen rills is everywhere heard. A grove
of aloes, orange-trees, laurels, fig-trees, evergreens,
pomegranates, jasmins, cacti, and I know not what
other growths, forms the approach to this exquisite
retreat. The gardens are terraced, and at the highest
point rises a belvedere from which you look down
upon the Generalife, the Alhambra, the city, and the
vast plain. This view is more comprehensive than that
from the bell-tower of the Alhambra, but not prefer-
able, for the sight of the Alhambra itself from above

is not edifying, the renaissance palace begun by Charles V being the most prominent object.

Granada is a place of surpassing interest and inexplicable charm. The situation is perfect, the associations romantic in the extreme, and the surroundings are remarkably picturesque. But to leave the place, one has to be awaked at three o'clock in the morning. We wrote in the visitors' book that we were " sorry to depart so early," which was doubly true. And if we heaved a Boabdillian sigh, it was with the thought of the long, hot ride to Cordova which was before us.

CHAPTER XV.

It is impossible to believe that in the time of the Moors, when their European dominion was seeing its palmiest days, Cordova — this sleepiest of cities, deep in a perpetual siesta — was a great metropolis, counting her inhabitants by the million and her mosques by the hundred. The only thing that seems real to the memory is the heat. At the Swiss Hôtel our room was on the ground floor; the sunlight was excluded by heavy wooden shutters; the floor was of brick; sweating jugs of water moistened the air; and there was plenty of soda-water in wheezy syphons to be had. But even in the patio the thermometer indicated a heat equal to 92° Fahrenheit, and the patio, with its fountain, marble pavement, and awnings on a level with the roof, was the coolest place in the house. The breeze which came from the street was like a blast from the furnace of an iron foundry. Even at night there was no relief, the mercury dropping only four or five degrees. One could do nothing but lie on a divan in one's shirt sleeves, read novels, smoke cigarettes, and wield a fan. No one in such a climate pretends to do any work. What few exertions are necessary are put forth in the early morning, before the sun has got fairly up, when the pavements and walls are giving out the least heat, and when a little shade can be found. In the course of a long walk down what must be one of the principal streets of the town, only a "solitary horseman" and a couple of priests are passed. The courtyard adjoining the mosque, with its orange-trees and inviting benches, affords a few diminutive spots of shade, which are monopolized by soldiers, priests, and beggars. It is a most grateful sensation to be met with a blast of cool, incense-laden air from the interior as you push back the leather-bound doors at the main portal.

This wonderful edifice, more curious than beautiful, is the chief pride of Cordova, and has been described by thousands of travelers. Every one feels instinctively that the Christians are intruders in it, for all the carved retablos and fantastic chapels in the world cannot alter the Moorish character. It was with this thought in mind that Heine pictured Almanzor ben Abdullah standing in "Cordova's grand cathedral," and mur-muring —

"O ye strong and giant pillars,
Once adorned in Allah's glory;
Now ye serve, and deck while serving,
The detested faith now o'er us."

What sort of an idea of the interior can be conveyed by stating that there are nineteen naves traversed by thirty-three others, sup- ported by over nine hundred columns of porphyry, jasper, breccia, and many-colored marbles? None at all, or at most a very faint one. Even when looking on such a thing it is impossible to " take it in " or appreciate it. This was the greatest Mussulman temple in the world, and in the time of the Moorish domination there were no less than fourteen hundred pillars, the ceiling was of sculptured cedar and larch, the walls were trimmed with marble, and eight hundred lamps lighted the vast edifice. " A sea of splendors," sang a poet, " filled this mysterious recess; the ambient air was impregnated

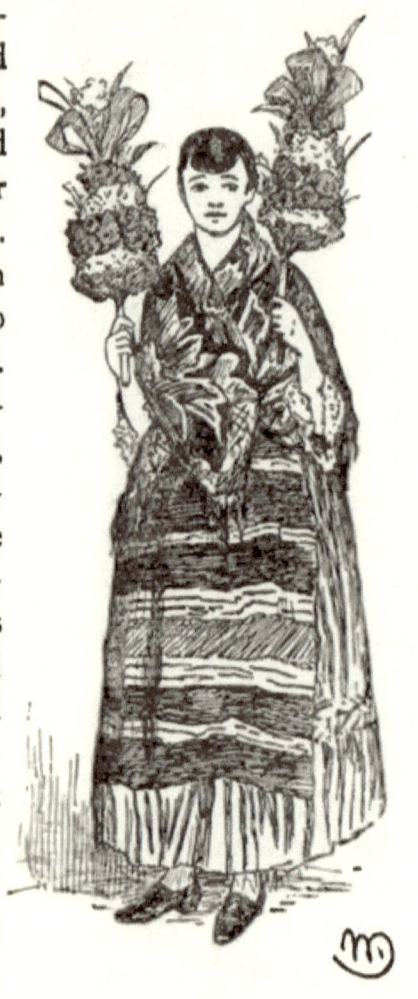

with aromas and harmonies, and the thoughts of the
faithful wandered and lost themselves in the labyrinth
of columns, which gleamed like lances in the sunshine."

Every one came to dinner at six o'clock, in the
flimsiest of toilettes, and there was a prodigious
fluttering of fans and clinking of ice in glasses and
fizzing of syphons. The conversation (we had learned
not a little Spanish by this time) concerned the
weather, and each gentleman stated how high his
particular thermometer had been during the day.
A party of English people who had just come from
Malaga cast a coolness over the company by alleging
that the mercury was at least ten degrees lower
(Fahrenheit) in that favored seaport. Almost every
one had been sleeping during the day, as is proper
and expedient. Late in the evening there began to
be some signs of life in the streets. We went out for
a walk, but found the pavements and white walls still
giving forth an intolerable heat. From the iron-grated
windows of the houses a draught of cold air rushed
out, laden with perfumes not precisely of Araby the
blest. The nursery rhyme of the bachelor who had
to take his wife home in a wheelbarrow on account
of the inconvenient narrowness of the thoroughfares
might have had an appropriate origin in Cordova.
The ways turn and twist in a very confusing fashion,
too. At midnight it began to be a little cooler, and
there were more people out than there had been at
any previous hour. This turning of night into day is

both novel and sensible. It is very convenient for the gallants and their Dulcineas, who, on opposite sides of a window-grating, exchange amorous glances and vows which may possibly be kept. Who knows?

CHAPTER XVI

BACK IN THE CAPITAL.

NORTHWARD, in the moonlit night, the long train swept leisurely across those wide and solemn uplands

A POT OF GARLIC

of La Mancha, while the bald-headed Spaniard in the opposite corner of the coupé purred the praises of Morpheus through his open mouth with a frightful regularity. At one station — it must have been long after midnight when we halted there — a party of pretty damsels was promenading up and down the long platform, enjoying the freshness of the night air, and when Hermano, forgetting that he had tied a white handkerchief over his head in lieu of a nightcap, thrust his head out of the window, there was an explosion of merry girlish laughter.

Madrid was hot, but not by any means so hot as Cordova, and it seemed quite homelike and comfortable. To a charming little darkened room on the Calle de Carmen the familiar strains of "Les Cloches de Corneville" came floating in at the balconied windows from a big Neapolitan hand-organ; the Puerta del Sol was as animated as ever; the people about the house spoke French; the horchata de chufas was as cool and refreshing as could be desired; the *Correspondencia* gave the latest news about the state of President Garfield's health and the French invasion of Tunis; and — last but not least — the pictures in the great gallery seemed to welcome us back like old friends. There were two New Yorkers at the Fonda de la Paz, a clergyman and a physician, who were quite discouraged by the heat, until we introduced them to a horchateria. The clergyman was undecided about going to a bull-fight on Sunday. He did not ask our advice, but we ventured to offer it gratuitously. Unfortunately one of us advised him to go, and the other counselled him to remain away, so that he was left in the same perplexed state of mind. I do not know what would have become of his conscience if it had not happened that one of the leading espadas was suddenly taken ill and the corrida was postponed from Sunday to Wednesday. The clergyman went. An Englishman was also among the new arrivals at the hôtel. He was a marine-surveyor, from Liverpool for Gibraltar, two days out, and had put in for repairs, as it were. Although his business took him to all parts of the earth, he did not speak any language but his own. He pronounced

Spain a miserable country, and the Spaniards miserable creatures. I quite won his heart by expressing my admiration for Gladstone, and before leaving the capital he made himself very agreeable to us, insisting on taking us to ride in the Retiro at his expense, probably to show his knowledge of the noble American custom of "treating." He continued to rail at the natives, ridiculed the powder and paint on the ladies' faces, and remarked pleasantly of the people whom he

GRENADES.

MADRID.

had met on the railroad, that he could "smell their 'ides." He further observed that he had his opinion of a people who called potatoes *patatas*. He had traveled in the United States, and took a great interest in President Garfield's condition, which was at that time thought to be hopeful. The secretary of the hôtel also discussed American politics with great profundity ; he thought that if the masses had their way Señor Blaine would be President. He informed us that the Southern Americans were much more intelligent than the Northerners, who were the *canalla*. By Southerners he meant, evidently, the inhabitants of South America. It may not be generally known here,

but it appears that the late war of the Rebellion was
between North America and South America. When
we were seated in the carriage, ready to start for a ride
after dinner, and the driver was waiting for the word,
our British friend turned to me, and said, gravely:—

"Tell 'im to *hallez*. That generally fetches 'em."

All foreign languages were the same to him, and
all foreigners also, probably. As we rode through
the Retiro, the driver, who spoke French, turned to
me and said the Princess's carriage was just ahead

of us. I urged him to catch up with it, so that we
might see the Princess; and he tried to do so, but in
vain. The Princess had two horses and we had but
one. "Ah, bah! monsieur," said our discomfited
driver, "eight legs are better than four."

I make a note of this remark to illustrate the Spanish fondness for shaping everything into epigrams and proverbial sayings. When I complained of the high price asked for berths on the sleeping-car, the good-humored response was that berths were " comme les petits gateaux ": in other words they were luxuries intended for those who could afford not to consider the petty question of money. And when I asked a Madrilenian whether the bulls were likely to be lively in a coming course, he replied that one could never tell about bulls, oranges, or women, until one had tried them.

CHAPTER XVII.

THE ESCORIAL.

DRIVEN by a false sense of duty, we undertook the arduous day's labor of seeing the "architectural nightmare" which forms such an appropriate monument to the most hateful of tyrants. Every one goes to the Escorial, and many pretend to admire it. The excursion is not very easy. It is necessary to quit Madrid at eight in the morning, and the chances are that you will not get back to town before half-past eight in the evening, though the distance is something less than thirty miles. To see the people, we took cheap excursion tickets, and went sweltering in a crowded car with soldiers, priests, women, babies, and great heaps of baskets, bundles, and bags. There was plenty of tobacco-smoke and conversation on the way. We rode from the station up to the Escorial village in an omnibus, and breakfasted very tolerably in the Fonda Miranda off egg soup (with plenty of oil, saffron, and pepper in it), a stewed forequarter of mule, a boiled fish of obscure origin, and a good pot of chocolate, with a bit of Burgos cheese, exhaling that same old familiar odor. The Fonda Miranda, in fact, is an "antiguo y acreditado establecimiento," in spite of the assaults of its rival, the Fonda de la Rosa, which announces that it is the " establecimiento inmediato al monasterio."

For several long hours we wandered about the Escorial, in a listless and depressed fashion, under the guidance of a matronly female who heroically defended us against the blandishments and wiles of the other guides. We had until then entertained a remote enmity to Felipe Segundo, but now we hated him with an active, intimate hatred, and believed the most malignant tales that ever were told of his cruelty and treachery. The whole vast pile is in full harmony with the character of its founder, whose heart was of granite, as cold and clammy as the touch of a reptile. Yet Philip's portraits do not make him look so hard as weak. He was of a light complexion, with a protruding lower lip, and calm gray eyes which have less of deviltry than of stupidity in them; and his neatly trimmed beard was worn in exactly the style in vogue at present in Paris. In the portrait by Pantoja, he is represented in a close-fitting black-velvet doublet, and holds in his white hands a chaplet.

> " Scarfs, garters, gold amuse his riper stage,
>   And beads and prayer-books are the toys of age."

That the monastery was built in the form of a gridiron, in honor of Saint Lawrence's warm martyrdom, is a widely diffused and interesting tradition, which may be true. But a gridiron is picturesque, nay statuesque, in comparison with the Escorial. A gridiron has some suggestiveness, some human interest, some warmth of style about it, as it were. Thus, a gridiron is far more beautiful than the Escorial, if not so large. After wandering about for a long time in the grim, great church, the chapels and the sacristy, the library and the pantheon, the palace and the galleries, we sat down to rest in one of the long cloisters, where we had a comfortable smoke in company with two jolly young monks, who could have given a lesson to Mark Tapley himself in the art of being cheerful under trying circumstances. The stone walls of the cloister were decorated with atrocious paintings of martyrdoms and tortures, battles and burnings. The seats were of stone, and long rows of square stone pillars stretched away on either hand. A small area of adventurous sunlight was visible near the centre of the enclosure, but everywhere else it was dark and chilly. Presently we visited the cell of one of the monks. It was about the size of a stateroom on an Atlantic steamship, but smelled sweeter, and maintained its *status quo* better. A scanty allowance of sunlight fell through the gratings of the little window and lay upon the bare floor. The walls were whitewashed neatly. A wooden bench and a couch of severe plainness, a little shelf bearing a crucifix and some books, were the only furnishings. There were several hundred cells precisely like this one, but few of them were occupied.   Their nakedness and poverty contrasted vividly with the superb appointments of the palace, not more than a stone's-throw distant, though even the fine tapestries and splendid inlaid woodwork of the royal apartments wore the melancholy aspect of abandoned glories.   In the chapter-house is a famous composition by Velasquez, " Jacob Receiving Joseph's Coat."   It was painted in Italy.   The figures are six in number and are literally copied from Spanish types of the day.   The design is notably good, and there is a very strong effect of light and shade.   Among other paintings carefully secluded here is Tintoret's "Washing of Feet," a dignified composition, with four or five distinct groups, making a total of more than a dozen figures, all of them interesting, against an architectural background. Luca Giordano's frescos are interesting ; and the Hall of Battles, with its mural paintings of half a dozen conflicts

on land and sea, is an amusing place.   A look at the squalid room where Philip ended his odious career, and where the visitor may still see his bed, table, desk, and chair,— relics which are as carefully preserved as the bones of any saint, — and we were quite ready to go, very well satisfied to get out into the fresh air, and bid farewell to the Escorial. We sauntered down through the gardens on the slope of the hill, and went through the Prince's house, a miniature palace full of interesting cabinet paintings. The train for Madrid was half an hour late when it rolled up to the Escorial station, and it stopped there one hour precisely, so that it arrived at Madrid an hour and a half behind time. This was such a common incident of travel that it occasioned little or no comment among the passengers. More soldiers, priests, women, babies, conversation, and smoke, — and at last we are back in Madrid, in time for dinner at the festive hour of nine P. M.

CHAPTER XVIII.

THE Art of Bull-fighting has its recognized laws, and an able exponent of its principles is *La Lidia*, a weekly periodical published in Madrid. It appears on the day following a bull-fight, with a detailed report of the affair, a criticism of the matadores, an editorial article on some subject connected with the ring, and a chromo-lithograph representing some torero in the act of making a difficult pass. It is amusing to see on what an elevated plane the writers place the Art. They talk of an espada being born and not made; of the difficulties and dangers of the profession; of its inexhaustible attractions to the genuine connoisseur; of the rewards of excellence in the arena; of the folly of entering into the race unless one is impelled by a real love of the Art; of the meanness of those who take it up merely to make money out of it; and of the boundless enthusiasm of the great masters now dead and gone, who won undying fame in the ring because to them the Arte taurino was a vocation, and they loved it. "Ah! there was Pepe Hillo, for instance — he was a thorough espada!" you can imagine them saying, with the reverence of a painter in speaking of Titian. The whole subject is regarded seriously as an art question, and they criticize a matador's every pass as closely as the French writers criticize the acting at the Théâtre Français. At the same time there is the element of Sport in it. It more than occupies the place given to horse-races or hunting in England, or base-ball in America. The spice of danger makes it a hundred-fold more exciting than anything of that sort. Accidents are of not uncommon occurrence, but they seldom prove fatal, and it is almost invariably held that if a torero is tossed by a bull it is his own fault. For example, Angel Pastor, a well-known Madrid espada, was seriously wounded on April 10, 1882, and *La Lidia* did not hesitate to declare that it was because of his lack of courage. The combat was the first regular corrida of the season, and Pastor took the place of Cara ancha, who had been injured the previous season. Pastor was dressed in a lilac-and-black suit; four bulls had been killed; the fifth was named Capirote; he was white and black, quick, wary, and cross-eyed. After the banderilleros had been dismissed, Pastor displayed his cloak to the beast, who came at him like a flash ("como una exhalacion"). Just when the fierce Capirote was within a few feet of him, Pastor was seen to change the cloak from one hand to another, leaving his body uncovered. He was caught and tossed by the bull, falling near the barrier with a severe wound in his right side. He tried to arise, but had to lean against the barrier, and was carried off to the infirmary by the assistants. The account does not state how the bull's attention was drawn away from the wounded man by the ever-alert chulos, but that is always taken for granted. Lagartijo at once entered the arena, and after eight beautifully finished passes, killed the redoubtable Capirote in superb style, amid tremendous cheers. Poor Angel Pastor, in the infirmary, could hear the loud shouts of applause which greeted his avenger. *La Lidia*, the next day, said of the wounded man that he was a torero of intelligence, who wielded his small cloak with great skill, and seemed to know what he was about, but added, "What a pity for him and for the Art that he has not more courage!" This was severe. Angel Pastor recovered, and two months after the accident he was ready to make his reappearance in the ring. It was June 11. His children, as *La Lidia* fancies, run to him to watch him as he makes his preparations, arranging his elaborate toilette, looking to his arms, polishing his swords. "The youngsters in playing about the room discover in a corner a forgotten silk vest, stained with blood, and with a round hole in the right side. The baby takes the garment, so lately bedewed with tears, and of it makes a lovely dress for her doll! The horses stamp impatiently outside the door where they are waiting to convey Papa Pastor to the Plaza de Toros. Friendly hands grasp his as he mounts, and as he proceeds shouts of enthusiastic welcome rend the air on every side; but amid the din he meditates, and his face remains grave. 'I alone am left to my children,' he says to himself, 'and I am now about entering a conflict which may make orphans of them.' Then, the sight of the vast plaza is horrible to him, and the bicolored banners fluttering so proudly at the tops of the tall staffs seem the auguries of Death."

"Can much be expected," asks *La Lidia*, "of one who in the presence of deadly peril allows a secret impulse of sentiment to weigh down his spirit? We believe not."

Then the writer goes on to consider the question in its broad aspects, as follows : —

"We would not," he says, "deprive the torero of his domestic affections; not at all; but, above and beyond these human ties, above and beyond these tender attachments and the various forms of sensibility, we conceive that there exists, and must exist, for the torero a glorious thing which for want of a better name we call *aficion!* Like the sailor who dares the fury of the ocean's billows, like the soldier who is first to bare his breast to the storm of bullets, so the *aficionado*

must take his Art for his only love, and not for a mere
employment, — as a cultivated passion, not for passing
gain ! "

Then he tells about Pepe Hillo, who, when suffering
térrible agonies from a wound, turned to his friends
and said (the first words that came from his fevered
lips), "When shall I be able to return to the ring?"
Another enthusiastic lidiador said, " Whenever I put
on my jacket and girdle my sash about me, I put my
wife away from me, run to the mirror to wipe the tears
from my face and there to remember that I am dressed
as a torero."

" What mean these words from the authoritative
lips of our glorious taurinas?" demands the eloquent
writer.   "They mean that, before our affections as
men, we should keep the line of duty firmly traced.
They mean that that torero is doubly in danger of
death who does not feel a *gran aficion*, a real passion,
for his perilous calling ; who does not prefer it to the
pleasures of home and all the modest affections of
life, and who does not feel that for him the Art is
a necessity."

Now all this rhetoric was *à propos* to poor Angel
Pastor, and was in very bad taste, besides being
misapplied, for when Pastor reappeared, he was
admirably brave, killed his two bulls with great
dexterity and coolness, and was rewarded with immense
applause.   However, what I have translated shows
very clearly the ground taken by the *Lidia* in all its

utterances. The plea of Art is ingeniously made in another essay, which points out that the competition of the ring is "a rivalry of forces, just as in all the other professions in life — a rivalry which stimulates and excites the noblest of passions: that is, the ambition of attaining to be worthy. To feel uplifted by this desire is equal to an extinction of all meanness. The struggle is not, then, censurable," etc. etc.

Are not these fine sentiments?

In another number of the *Lidia* we find a careful and elaborate study of Frascuelo and Lagartijo, the two leading espadas of Spain. Frascuelo and Lagartijo are *noms de guerre*, the real names of these mighty heroes being Salvador Sanchez and Raphael Molina. All Madrid is divided into two partisan camps respecting the merits of these rival stars. Frascuelo probably is the greater man; at least he wears the largest brilliants on his embroidered shirtfront and is followed about in the Puerta del Sol by the more numerous escort of admirers. A harder looking hero it would be difficult to find. He is of medium height, slight, of swarthy complexion, with curly gray hair; and his bearing has all the studied elegance and dignity of one who knows himself worthy of the adoration he receives. A wide-brimmed hat is artistically adjusted on one side of his head, and a gorgeous silken sash encircles his waist. Thus arrayed, he spends the greater part of his time on weekdays loafing in the Café Imperial and its vicinity, surrounded by a troop of friends who

are proud of the privilege of "treating" him, anxious
to guffaw at his slightest joke, and eager to hear with
solemn attention the words of wisdom that fall from
his lips.   The whole week is only too short a time in
which to discuss last Sunday's bull-fight and prophesy
as to next Sunday's performance.   ·As a torero, Frascuelo is brave to the point of rashness, and has many
a time seemed to invite death with a smiling face.
"He invites the bulls with fine and elegant delibera-
tion; handles his *muleta*, if not like a great master,
splendidly at times; and gives the finishing-stroke as
few fencers could, even among the most famous in
former days."   Note the reverential tone of the
distinction in favor of the old masters.   In spite of
Frascuelo's skill and coolness, he was once tossed
by a bull named Guindaleto, in Madrid.   The city was
in a ferment; and the greatest concern was manifested.
But when he recovered from his wounds, a reaction
took place, and he was so unpopular for a time that it
was proposed to expel him from the Court.   However,
he reappeared in the arena one fine day, and conducted himself with such brilliant daring, and such
exceptional skill, that he reconquered the approbation
of the people, who are ever ready to forgive any fault
but cowardice. ·

Besides Frascuelo and Lagartijo, there are minor
pets of the populace, —El Gallo (Fernando Gomez),
Cara ancha (José Sanchez del Campo), José Machía,
Felipe García, Angel Pastor, and others, — for each

town has its own favorites. El Gallo (The Cock) is a graduate of the famous Sevillian school of toreros. It was in the historic ring of the Andalusian metropolis that he made his reputation, and the manner of it, as related by the *Lidia*, was as follows : —

He jumped into the arena one day when he had no right to be there, and, walking to the very centre of the vast ring, looked about in an unconcerned way, drew a white handkerchief from his pocket, placed it on the ground carefully, and knelt upon it. Thereupon the public began to shout "Out with him!" "Take him to jail!" "He'll be killed!" But the young man, paying no attention to the outcry, called to the bull and threw his hat into the air. The beast turned, and on seeing this odd figure kneeling, he darted toward it like a flash.

The audience gave a cry of horror.

A second later, and fright was changed into enthusiastic and ecstatic admiration!

What had happened?

El Gallo, mocking the fury of the bull as he charged, had received the terrible beast on his sword there as he knelt, with his breast almost touching the animal's head, and, rising unhurt, with the handkerchief in one hand, the hat in the other, he smiled with serene self-possession! Such audacity is not approved by the genuine lidiadores, who are careful to applaud only the recognized and orthodox practices of the Art. But the Spanish public adores courage in any form.

Sevilla, a famous picador, once attacked a bull out of his turn, and the people shouted " A fuera Sevilla ! a ti no te toca ! lo demasiado bueno es malo." His horse was terribly gored, having turned to escape the bull, and " the first use which Sevilla made of his legs, on regaining them, was to bestow as hearty a kick as the encumbrance of his armor would allow, upon the uplifted head of the poor animal. This proof of his unshaken courage and presence of mind, as well as of his brutality, was received with immense applause." *

So quick are the motions of the men and the bull that sometimes it is impossible to tell how the toreros escape, and, on the other hand, sometimes it is equally impossible to know how it is that an accident happens. José Candido, who was a celebrated matador of the last century, met with a terrible death. A bull of unusual ferocity and cunning happened to be in the ring, and followed up one of the picadores with such persistency that Candido interposed to save the man's life. During this episode Candido either slipped or threw himself down purposely to avoid the beast's blow — at all events he was seen stretched on the ground. The bull jumped over him, and turned very rapidly ; in an instant he was caught up and tossed, being horribly gored several times in succession. He was lifeless when picked up by his aids. The sketch of his career ends with a particular mention of

---

* Ridell, " Spain Revisited."

the circumstance that he invented a certain way of jumping over the bull's head.

The ordinary performances are often varied by the introduction of novel and fantastic features. Among the memorable occasions in the Madrid arena was a fight between a bull and several beasts of prey — a lion, a tiger, and twenty-eight bull-dogs. The bull was the victor. The dogs ran away from him. Another very curious combat was that between a bull and an enormous elephant. The bull rushed upon his adversary, who immediately seized him with his trunk, lifted him on his tusks and threw him a distance of ten yards, after which he quietly stepped on him and crushed the life out of him.

CHAPTER XIX.

In Bayonne, — street of Thiers, — in front of St. Stephen Hôtel. Sitting there in the early evening, while the breeze that heralded a coming thunder-shower swept clouds of dust down the street, we were, it must be confessed, glad to be back in France. It has been written in the books that Bayonne has a Spanish character. However this may be, it is not noticed by the traveler just out of Spain. A few Spanish signs, a few Spanish tourists in the hôtels, and the Basque dialect of the inhabitants, may remind one of Spain; but the town is thoroughly French in its appearance, and there is nothing Spanish about the quick movements and smartness of those young women seen trooping one after another to the public pump at the street corner, and bearing away heavy jugs of clear water in all directions. The French women are certainly admirable in their thrift and industry. How many of them take hold of business either independently or with their husbands, and with what success! They are as keen as two-edged blades, and it would be hard to find a parallel in any other nation for the practical capacity of a certain class of shop-keeping females, — cashiers, clerks, saleswomen, landladies, accountants, etc., — who are everywhere at work in France, very often as proprietors even, shouldering heavy responsibilities, and putting the men to the blush by their tact and energy. There is nothing Spanish about yonder passing squad of red-trousered soldiers, all out of step, marching to the sound of a ringing *fanfare* of bugles; for, alas! the drum has been abolished in the French army. There is nothing Spanish about the waiter flitting in and out of the door of the café near by, with his long-handled coffeepot in one hand and the other ready for *pourboires;* he wears slippers tied with ribbons, a short black jacket, and a long white apron, and never, by any chance, is there any headgear covering his close-cut locks, though customers will sit outdoors on days when one would suppose their very teeth must chatter.

Bayonne is a very interesting and delightful old town. It has buildings dating from the sixth century, yet it has kept pace with the times in enterprise, and is to-day commercially prosperous. Its citadel is one of Vauban's famous works. In a little valley to the north of it lie the bones of many Englishmen who died while besieging the place in 1814. The one fact that everybody knows about Bayonne is that bayonets originated here. The city, though often besieged, has never been taken; and it refused to participate in the massacre of St. Bartholomew. The small River Nive here flows into the broad Adour, which is spanned by a handsome stone bridge and empties into the Bay

of Biscay only a few miles below the town. The
Adour at this point is a nobly picturesque stream, and
below Bayonne the banks are wooded and hilly, so
that it looks like several American rivers that might
be named. The shallows near the mouth are great
obstacles to the commerce of the town. European
rivers are so often mere insignificant creeks in comparison with the great rivers in the United States, that
I always relish the anecdote of the Yankee who stood
on London bridge, and said, with intense scorn: "And
this dirty creek is what they call the grand old Father
Thames!" Bayonne is the largest town of the
department of the Basses Pyrénées, a politically
perverse region, whose antecedents are of the greatest
interest. On the north it adjoins Les Landes, a
dreary waste of sandy country where Rosa Bonheur
found her picturesque shepherds on stilts and made
them familiar the world over. The department was
a portion of the ancient realm of Béarn and Navarre,
prominent in history; and a part of it is included in
what was of old the country of the Basques, that
extraordinary race whose origin no one can trace, and
whose characteristics are said to survive all the
mutations of wars, conquests, political distinctions,
and social innovations. What is strange about the
French peasants of this region is the fact that they
are decidedly Spanish in character and customs. The
Spaniards of the other side of the mountains are
apparently not affected by French influences. It is

curious, because one would naturally suppose the weaker people must be the more susceptible to foreign influence. The French built all the railways in Northern Spain and are introducing business in many of the towns there, but their presence does not affect the unique qualities of the people. The Basques are said to have descended straight from Adam, — that is to say, straighter than the rest of us, — but it is doubtful if they have any more of the old Adam in them than those whose lineage is more obscure. From this famous little corner of Europe came Henry of Navarre, the Bernadotte family, and Orthès, who was prefect when Bayonne refused to participate in the massacre of St. Bartholomew. The peasants still wear on their heads the *bérets* of dark-blue stuff, which somewhat resemble sailors' hats and are very useful as well as becoming; and the rustic women who toil in the fields preserve their effective and picturesque bright-hued costumes, such as may be seen excellently in Julien Dupré's paintings. This department includes, besides Bayonne and Biarritz, the world-renowned mountain resort of Pau, and the less widely known watering-places of Eaux-Bonnes and Eaux-Chaudes away up in the mountains. Lourdes, the locality of the grotto famed throughout Catholic Christendom for the miraculous apparition of the Holy Virgin, is not far away in the neighboring department of the Upper Pyrenees, which contains a dozen prominent mountain resorts, such as Bagnères de Bigorre and Bagnères de

Luchon, the future rivals of the most favored centres of travel in Switzerland.

Biarritz was made a fashionable resort by the caprice of the Empress Eugénie, who was fond of the locality, but it is not a superlatively attractive place. A good many Spanish go there to get cool in summer, and a good many English go there to get warm in winter ; but as it is rather warm in summer and decidedly rainy and breezy most of the winter, it is questionable if either class of habitués meets with entire success. The hôtels are enormous, gaudy, and very expensive, and there is, of course, a big casino. The beach is not to be compared for a moment with that of any first-class American seaside resort. But the water has the capacity of assuming the most exquisitely beautiful shades of green and blue imaginable. This peculiarity of the Bay of Biscay is observed all along the coast, from Arcachon (a very swell resort farther north, only an hour's ride from Bordeaux) down to the Spanish watering-place of San Sebastian, memorable for having been sacked and burned by the English, under Wellington, in 1813. Biarritz is mildly interesting to the casual visitor, but nothing more; and there must always hang about the place certain unpleasant associations with the flashy court of Napoléon the Little. Between Biarritz and Bayonne, which are only five miles apart, there is not only the main line of railway but also a narrow-gauge road. The cars are furnished with seats on top, like some of the suburban lines around Paris. There is also a fine carriage-road, lined with handsome villas belonging to a select assortment of counts, marquises, etc., not omitting that sort of " self-made man " who adores his maker — the French type so well represented by the immortal M. Poirier in Augier's comedy.

The low country immediately north of the Pyrenees is uncommonly beautiful and fertile. From Bayonne up to Pau the railway goes through a succession of charming scenes, which become more and more diversified and interesting as the train nears the ancient capital of the province, following along almost the entire distance the rapid stream known as the Gave de Pau. At length, on the right, the foothills of the Pyrenees are overtopped, one after another, by gigantic snow-peaks, which, by the time Pau is reached, form an almost continuous line of dazzling white along the southern horizon.

No one who has visited Pau — this famous winter resort — will be disposed to dispute the assertion that it is one of the most favored spots in the world, or to deny that the panorama from the terrace is hardly to be equaled in Switzerland. The combination of attractions which makes Pau what it is, must continue to draw increasing numbers of visitors there every year. Added to the wonderfully equable climate, it is a social centre of no ordinary calibre, possessing all the refinements and luxuries of an old and thriving capital, and a situation which for picturesqueness can-

not be surpassed by any place similarly accessible.
The hôtels are superlatively good — as good as those
of Lucerne or Lausanne ; all of them command that
glorious view to the southward ; and at present it is
almost impossible to obtain accommodations during
the season at prices within the means of any but mil-
lionaires.   It is the natural centre of a superb region,
a smiling country of verdure and constant bloom.   For
miles along the macadamized rural highways one may
pass between estates which vie with each other in
elegance.   Jurançon, the principal suburb, which lies
just across the river, is a town of wealthy grandees
whose villas and castles dot the slopes of beautiful
green hills as far as the eye can reach.   The city itself
has thirty thousand inhabitants, a picture-gallery, public library, school of design, theatre, casino, and " all
the improvements."   It is tremendously gay in winter,
if there can be said to be any winter, and in the modish
crowd not a few English and Americans are found.
In the old quarters of the town, which lies high and
dry on a platform forty metres above the river, there
are plenty of "bits" which would delight the soul of an
artist ; tall old houses with tiny windows and quaint
roofs, all jumbled together and surmounted by a forest
of comical chimney-pots, which leaves even Edinburgh
in the shade.   The castle of Henry IV, on the brink
of the plateau, has six square towers, some of them
nearly covered with ivy, and fits into the view as if it
had grown there.   The wide moat which formerly

separated it from the town is now an alley planted
with trees. The largest tower, named after Gaston
Phébus, was used as a prison under Louis XIV.
There were secret cells also below the Montaüzet
tower, — *oubliettes*. What a significant name ! The
chief object of interest in the castle is " our Henry's "
cradle, a tortoise-shell. During the Reign of Terror
the people wished to destroy this memorial of royalty.
The governor of the castle cunningly substituted a
false tortoise-shell cradle for the real one, and the citi-
zens burned the counterfeit with just as much joy.*
The best of republicans in France nowadays are too
shrewd to destroy any objects which possess historic
interest enough to attract the notice of tourists.

Of foreign tourists Pau sees comparatively few, but
the winter population includes a host of fashionable
English people, who have here their own libraries,
clubs, churches, cemetery, cricket, polo, and lawn-
tennis grounds, etc. The Museum of the Infant Don
Sebastian of Bourbon and Braganza contains over
seven hundred paintings, among which there are two
Titians, five Murillos, six Salvator Rosas, five Goyas,
six Riberas, two Rubens, two Teniers, and one each of
Velasquez, Van Dyck, Rembrandt, etc. The Museum

---

* " Pendant la Terreur, le berceau de Henri IV fut soustrait à la rage de la populace, qui avait
envahi le château pour livrer aux flammes les objets qui rappelaient la royauté. Le commandant
du château, M. d'Espalungue d'Arros, résolut de remplacer le berceau du grand roi par une cara-
pace d'égale grandeur, que M. de Beauregard avait dans son cabinet d'histoire naturelle. Un
homme dévoué, le sergent Lamaignère, gardien du château, opéra cette substitution. Une cara-
pace ordinaire fût donc brûlée sur la place publique, tandis que le véritable berceau était transporté
sous la toiture de la maison Beauregard, où il resta caché, pendant plusieurs années." — *Saget*,
Description du Château de Pau, 1838.

of Pau has some valuable historical works, but contains
little to interest the passing tourist.

The panorama of the distant mountains is a source
of constant surprise and pleasure, for with every vari-
ation of light, with every change in the disposition·of
the clouds, from morning till night, it is undergoing
the most marvelous transformations. It seems unreal;
you sit out on that terrace hour after hour, and try to
grasp it, to realize it, but it is useless. At your feet
the shallow stream ripples over its rocky bed; the
straggling town of Jurançon, at first a compact mass,
then disintegrating into multitudes of detached villas,
lifting their slate roofs above the trees from among their
parks and lawns, next catches the eye; then undulating
meadows lead your glance onward to a line of hills —
the *côteaux* with their vineyards; farther yet, and a
second, higher chain of wooded hills; in the blue distance, hazy and soft in outline; and, beyond these, the
vast towering summits of the snow-peaks, now hidden
and now revealed by the shifting clouds: not one or
two, or a dozen peaks, but scores of them, rounded
and sharp, low and high, near and far, an unbroken line
of gleaming monarchs from east to west, with the
magnificent Pic du Midi in the very centre of the chain,
directly in front of you, lording it over all the rest.

CHAPTER XX.

FORTY-FOUR kilometres away, among those lofty mountains, are the two rival health resorts of Eaux-Bonnes and Eaux-Chaudes, whose mineral springs are highly esteemed by wheezy sufferers from catarrh, the hoarse-voiced victims of bronchial difficulties, and the irritable martyrs to rheumatism. To go to either of these places it was necessary to take the daily diligence from Pau, hire a private conveyance at twenty-five or thirty francs a day, or — best of all — to take to Shanks's mare. The route is over an excellent national road, such as is found only in France, and is in a very interesting part of the mountain region. But the railway was (1881) already in process of construction, and the entire district will soon be accessible to the hordes of travelers who don't go where there are no railroads, and the sort of creatures who consider riding up the Righi or Mount Washington a glorious feat. For my part I am

always glad to have visited such isolated and grand
regions before the "iron horse" has planted his cloven
hoof on them.

In meandering southward from Pau, the first village
of consequence that we passed through was Gan, a
squalid and pent-up town, with houses of immense
antiquity and equally great filth and ugliness. Then
we came to Rébénacq, and found the village enjoying
its annual fête. It was a scene that could not fail to
recall to mind vividly the paintings of Dutch village
festivals by Teniers. From the bench where we sat,
in front of a humble café situated on the large square,
we watched the young men and women dancing in the
open air. The three musicians who composed the
orchestra sat in chairs placed on the top of a table, and
played one and the same tune over and over again
with never-failing gusto. It was evidently the tune
which caused the death of the ancient bovine. The
dances were quadrilles, and they had a certain grace
and dignity of their own. At the conclusion of each
set the men " turned their partners " most vigorously,
putting both hands around the waist and then lifting
the women up about a foot into the air. Some of the
girls were very pretty. They were dressed in their
best, and the men even wore " biled shirts," in several
instances. The enjoyment of all hands was hearty.
The doors of the church stood open, and occasionally
a party of the convives would enter and go through
with their devotions. Among the gayest of the giddy

throng were a lot of black pigs who went wandering
about the square and afforded amusement to the children who caressed them and teased them alternately.
The old people sat knitting, drinking, eating, gossiping,
and looking on, in the shade of the stone barracks at
one side of the *place*. A few steps beyond Rébénacq
we saw the wonderful Oueil du Néez (or eye of the
Néez), which is a refreshing spectacle of a hot day;—
it is the river gushing out from its subterranean caverns
into the light of day and flowing down to give its
water-supply to Pau, over twenty kilometres distant;
and it resembles an immense spring boiling out of the
wooded hillside. After passing through two or three
unimportant villages, the traveler shortly pulls up at
Louvie for lunch and a rest. This place is just at the
entrance of the beautiful valley of the Ossau, a long,
flat farming district, entirely shut in by high hills and
mountains, a little world by itself, with some seventeen
villages and seven thousand inhabitants, all farmers,
who wear the old costumes and " run things " on the
patriarchal plan, according to their notions. Louvie
might pass as a fair sample of a Spanish post-village.
The low whitewashed stone tavern is built around a
square court, paved with cobble-stones and redolent of
the odors of the stable, and from a canopied interior
balcony running around this hot and glaring court
come the voices of a bevy of young women, ostensibly
sewing, but really flirting with the drivers and travelers
below. Out in the narrow, dusty street is a group of

hideous, deformed beggars, who catch your eye when you come to a front window to look at the view, and smile, and beckon, and hold out their hats, and exhibit their sores — all in full sight of a blue-and-white sign

which says, "Mendicity is forbidden in this Department." The main entrance to the inn is through a brick-floored hallway adjoining the kitchen, where a glimpse of the fat cook mopping his perspiring brow, and enveloped in clouds of smoke and steam, serves to give the wayfarer an appetite for his *déjeûner*. Everything about the place is suggestive of heat, dirt, and hopeless shiftlessness.

Beginning with Louvie, the valley of the Ossau extends southward about fifteen kilometres to the town of Laruns. It is hemmed in on all sides by mountains, and the scenery all along it is marvelously fine. Queer villages are seen here and there nestling high up on the flanks of the mountains. Ruined castles and churches crown the summits of rocky hills rising from the broad, flat bottom of the valley. At Bielle, the ancient capital of the district, there are several ruins of Roman constructions and some famous old fifteenth-century houses. Beyond Laruns, which is the largest town in the valley, and whose public square we immediately recognized as an old acquaintance, the highway forks, the road to the right

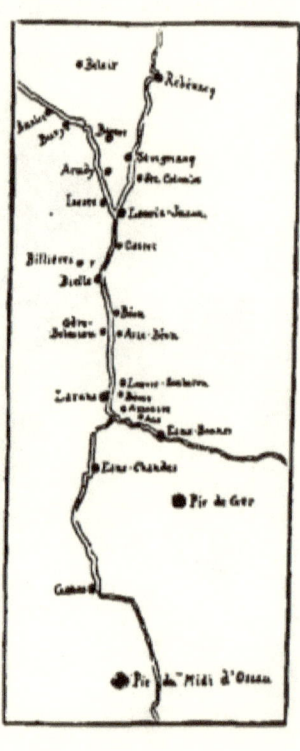

going to Eaux-Chaudes, and that to the left going to Eaux-Bonnes. This is the end of the valley. The road to Eaux-Bonnes zigzags up a long and steep incline, entering the narrow and precipitous valley of the Valentin; and before long the weary traveler enters the place of his destination, probably shut in on all sides by a thick curtain of clouds.

CHAPTER XXI

EAUX-BONNES.

EAUX-BONNES, in point of situation, is one of the most delightfully odd places in the world. We at once named it "the jumping-off place," and were rather astonished, when the fog lifted, to find that there was anything beyond. "I am confident," said Hermano, looking about the room with the radiant air of a discoverer, "that we have at last found a place where Americans do not come. We are probably the first Yankees who ever found their way into this remote and unheard-of corner of the world." As he ceased speaking he pulled open a bureau drawer, and with a groan of discouragement lifted from it an old, torn copy of the New York *Herald!*

The village, if not the authentic jumping-off place of our youthful dreams, affords abundant opportunities for saltatorial suicides. It is perched on a narrow ledge overhanging a deep gorge, and can never grow much larger than it is now unless some new devices in the way of aerial dwellings are invented. But it has its public square, — as what French town has not? — a very steep little park, where you must be careful not to tumble down, for you might roll several miles

before you could pick yourself up again. A most
industrious, loud, and indefatigable band plays during
the afternoon and evening, and from the half-dozen
hôtels there emerges a well-dressed crowd of genteel
invalids to take the air and enjoy the social opportunities at hand. About ten thousand visitors come here
every year. There is something irresistibly attractive
about mineral-waters to a Frenchman, and if one
fancies himself an invalid nowadays, all he thinks
necessary to a complete restoration of health is
unlimited guzzling of, and bathing in, bad-tasting and
worse-smelling spring water. The "establishment,"
as the big building where the water is dispensed is
called, is the most important edifice of the town.

The walks about the neighborhood are full of
romance and attraction ; it is a region of beautiful
cascades. Among a half-dozen of them, quite near
the village, the finest is the Cascade du Gros Hêtre.
An American is apt to be rather scornful concerning
foreign waterfalls, but there is no humbug about this
one ; it is a beauty. The tremendous volume of
water that comes thundering down some sixty feet
into a deep pool almost shakes the earth round about,
and casts off immense clouds of spray, which, accumu-
lating on the foliage of the big beech-tree overhanging
the chasm, drips continually in a gentle shower on
the moss-covered rocks and into the seething eddies
of the stream below. Nothing could be more romantic
than the Promenade de l'Impératrice, along whose

sinuosities you stroll in going to this cascade. It
follows the left flank of the wild and deep gorge
through which the Gave du Valentin tumbles and
rumbles, and sings and roars, and leaps from shelf
to shelf of its rocky bed on its way to the peaceful
valley of the Ossau. When we walked there the
clouds were all about us, and the woods were filled
with the mysterious yet significant voices of the
unseen waters. Other cascades big enough to be
dignified by titles, besides the Gros Hêtre, are the
Serpent, the Discoo, and the Eaux-Bonnes. These
are all on the same stream, which is but a succession
of waterfalls. But there are arduous and adventurous
excursions which can be made from Eaux-Bonnes,
which is a resort for climbers as well as for invalids,
and which is quite a centre for guides. The Pyrenean
guides are not reputed to be very skilful, by the way,
though there must be some exceptions. The great
excursion from this point is to the Pic de Ger, an
ascent which can be made in one day by putting in
eight or ten hours of good, stiff work. The view is
extensive and very fine, and the climb is not so dangerous as it is tiresome. However, the most agreeable
by far of all the excursions, and that affording the best
views at the least expense of effort, is the trip from
Eaux-Bonnes to Eaux-Chaudes over the Gourzy, an
affair of only three or four hours, on foot or on horseback, with or without guides. The Gourzy is a high
plateau commanding an exceptionally broad panorama.

Anybody who is fond of going down hill on horseback may adopt that method of locomotion ; but for this excursion all others will do well to walk, in spite of the blandishments of the guides, who, in almost every case, own horses and are naturally anxious to let them.

CHAPTER XXII.

THE French guidebooks of Adolphe and Paul Joanne are unsatisfactory works in many respects, and that to the Pyrenees is no exception, yet it is so much better than nothing, that it would be an error to travel without it. The faculty of making a good guidebook (which is a sort of sixth sense, like that of "keeping an hôtel ") seems to belong pre-eminently to the unrivaled and immortal Baedeker, and it is a great pity he has never covered the ground which includes the Pyrenees. A tour through this region must be planned on a different principle from that adopted in the Alps, owing to the peculiar configuration of the range. Instead of going from place to place in a continuous progress, as can be done in Switzerland, you must take up your headquarters in certain centres here long enough to

explore the surroundings, for railways are rare, and
good diligence-roads are only found in the low, broad
valleys on the French side.   These centres are as
follows : Eaux-Bonnes, **Eaux-Chaudes**, Cauterets, **Luz,
Baréges, Bagnères de** Bigorre, **Bagnères de** Luchon,
and one or two minor points frequented by climbers,
such as **Aulus, Ax,** and **Le** Vernet.   It would be
stretching a point to say that the scenery rivals that of
the Alps, which for grandeur and diversity of forms
has no equal anywhere, and never can have.   But the
Pyrenees have a character all of their own, and are all
the more interesting in that they are unlike other
mountains.   The places just mentioned as centres for
mountain excursions are almost invariably health
resorts, renowned for their mineral-springs, and most
of them are situated at great elevations, remarkable
for picturesque surroundings, either nestling on the
borders of wild and romantic gorges, or hemmed in on
all sides by huge mountains at the end of some lateral
valley.   The place in the Rhone valley, called Leuker-
bad, in German, and Louèche-les-bains, in French,—
a resort which has been "written to death,"— is, in
respect to situation as well as character, very similar to
some of these Pyrenean villages.   It must be said to
the credit of the Pyrenees, that if they have no such
beautiful lakes as there are in Switzerland, they are
equally devoid of English and German tourists.

From Eaux-Bonnes the traveler naturally turns his
steps towards Eaux-Chaudes, only nine kilometres

distant, in the narrow valley of the Gave d'Ossau. Descending to the broad, open valley of the Ossau near Laruns, the road to the left is taken, and immediately you find yourself in the Gorge du Hourat, one of the

most striking defiles in the region. On either side of the stream the sheer precipices tower to a height of several hundred feet, almost shutting out the light of day, and the road is cut in the rock on the right bank, forming a long gallery about one hundred and twenty

feet above the torrent.   At one point a bridge spans
the raging little river, and here a pathway leads down
to the water, so that you can run down there and get
the effect of the tremendous twin cliffs from below.
Those who have seen the Via Mala in Switzerland (or,
as A. Ward used to say, "Those of you who have
been in jail") know what a fascination there is about
such places.   The traces of an old road, now disused,
are seen on the other side of the defile, and the spot
is indicated where a horse and carriage and beautiful
young lady went off the brink, one dark night, and
plunged into the abyss.   The unfortunate young
woman's name escapes me, but there is a delicious
story about her disappointment in love, or something
of that sort, — which I have also forgotten, — always
related by the guides in a touching manner.   The
trouble is that each guide has built up a " revised version " of the anecdote to suit his own notions of the
thrillingly romantic.   If the truth were known, it may
be that only a drunken pedlar and his donkey fell into
the gulf.   If this be denounced as an unworthy suspi-
cion, all that can be said is that the guides ought to
organize a synod and agree as to what story shall be
told about the antecedents and title of the beauteous
victim

It was raining at Eaux-Chaudes when the elegant
and gentlemanly landlord of the principal inn said, in
what he flattered himself was pure English, " Good-
morning ! " and when we said, in what we knew was

classic French, "*Bong joor!*" It was raining, but
the water was not warm. The morning had been of
that tantalizing sort that keeps a mountaineer in a
state of indecision as to his programme. It rained a
little occasionally, and then it made a feint of clearing
off, the clouds rolled up higher on the mountain sides,
and opened here and there, exposing a suggestive
patch of snow in about the place where the zenith
ought to be. In any other locality than the mountains
it would have cleared off. Once the sun came out,
and a rent in the clouds showed us a whole glittering
pinnacle of ice startlingly near us, almost overhead;
but in ten minutes more the heavy mist came rolling
down the valley, shutting down suddenly, and shortly
followed by a fresh shower. We wanted to go to the
Plateau, beyond Gabas the neighboring settlement,
and the last town in France, for the purpose of
obtaining the superb view of the Pic du Midi to be
got there; and every one who has been in the
mountains (or in jail) can appreciate the impatience
with which we stood drumming on the window-panes
and murmuring gentle imprecations on the weather.
There were no other guests in the hôtel, if I remember
aright, and the usual collection of torn guidebooks,
dogeared Tauchnitz editions of "British" authors
(including Fenimore Cooper and Bret Harte), and
one or two French novels, formed a slim capital on
which to beguile any great amount of time away.
Consequently, the inevitable resort of man in time

of *ennui* (which is French) was taken, and we ordered
a lunch. The dining-room proved to be a remarkably
amusing place. The walls were decorated with
paintings, almost life-size, of the Pic du Midi, the
Gorge du Hourat, the cave of Eaux-Chaudes, the
Pic de Ger, and of various other objects of interest
in the neighborhood. Such works of art were never
seen surely anywhere else. Such color, such drawing,
such effects of perspective, such chiaroscuro! If
laughter aids digestion, then these masterpieces of
local genius are rightly placed. The mute, inglorious
Michael Angelo of the village saw his opportunity
here, and grasped the skirts of happy chance to some
effect. When Eaux-Chaudes is dug up from under
the débris of the Pic de Ger, in 2883, the future man
will be a good deal more astonished than any of the
excavators of Pompeii have been.

Eaux-Chaudes is almost as picturesque in point
of situation as Eaux-Bonnes. It lies in so narrow
a gorge that there is just room for the single street
which runs along one side of the Gave d'Ossau. The
thermal establishment is a big square structure,
utilizing three of the springs. There are but two
hôtels, and these are cheaper than any of the half-
dozen at Eaux-Bonnes, for the visitors here are fewer
and less fashionable. A visit to the cave is one of
the first duties of the newly arrived traveler. And
he may rest assured that it is well worth seeing.
Leaving the village, and climbing along a steep bridle-

path for about an hour, you come to the mouth of the cave, where you stop to put on your overcoat and await the preparations of the fantastic custodian who lives in a hut at the entrance. This wild-eyed ogre, who insists on taking in Bengal-lights at your expense for the purpose of illu-minating the interior properly, salutes you with great dignity and

looks at you with an are-you-prepared-to-die expres-sion, but turns out to be harmless and rather loqua-cious. He unlocks the gate (the slats make the exterior of the wonder look like an extemporized henhouse) and lights a big, dripping pine-knot torch, which he flourishes about as he leads the way over the slippery, slimy rocks into the uncanny hole. Presently the cave narrows, and the floor-space becomes con-tracted, so that before long you find yourself trudging over a rapid torrent on a narrow footbridge, whose solitary and shaky handrail you grasp with a good deal of caution. It is about at this point that the ogre, without any warning whatsoever, gives an unearthly whoop to show off the echoes. A diabolical chorus of diminishing howls mocks his shout and mingles with the roar of the furious stream. Then the ogre fires off

his Bengal-fuses, and makes visible the most frightful
scene imaginable — a world of rocky and watery
desolation which appalls the imagination and makes
one thank God for the fresh air and warmth and
sunlight of the earth's surface.   The cave is four hundred and fifty metres deep, and is closed to further
exploration by a subterranean cascade coming from a
fissure which is believed to communicate with a plateau
some thousand feet above, where the waters from the
Pic de Ger are ingulfed.   In walking these four hundred
and fifty metres, you cross and recross the stream
about eight times, and there must be a good deal of
danger, for there is nowhere more than a single rail
to take hold of, and the rotten planks on which you
go are as slippery as ice, owing to the accumulated
moisture and slime.   The man who falls from one
of these bridges may as well give up making any
codicils to his will, for the rocks are crusted thickly
with slime, and the stream has depths which are
treacherous and horrible to the view.   Altogether the
cave of Eaux-Chaudes is a frightful as well as a
wonderful place.

CHAPTER XXIII.

THE PLATEAU OF BIOUS-ARTIGUES.

A START was made for Gabas as soon as it was thought that the weather would permit an excursion to the Plateau of Bious-Artigues, whence that famous view of the Pic du Midi d'Ossau was to be obtained. Gabas is eight kilometres beyond Eaux-Chaudes, to the southward, and occupies the pent-up extremity of the same little valley. It is only a hamlet, consisting of an inn and a half-dozen houses or so, an old church, and a marble quarry. It is eleven hundred and twenty-five metres above the sea level, and is the point of departure for several arduous mountain excursions. Here the highway comes to an end, and a rough mountain-road winds upward through an elevated and wild pass leading over to Panticosa, in Spain. It was stated that a walk of an hour and a half, along a bridle-path which follows the right bank of the Gave de Bious, would bring us to a certain sawmill located on the Plateau of Bious-Artigues. So we left Gabas at noon, and counted on employing the whole afternoon in a delightful excursion. The path was very plain for the first two or three miles, and a succession of extremely picturesque views made the way seem only too short. Unhappily the weather was as fickle as it commonly is in the mountains, and everything was soon cloaked in an impenetrable mist. After an hour and a half of sturdy exercise, the conviction was gradually forced upon us that we had lost our way. At this time we were crossing some swampy uplands where cattle were grazing, and, having almost lost the faint trail several times, we were about to turn back, when we found a narrow corduroy road leading up into the woods. This

was evidently used for the purpose of hauling timber

down from the mountains, and it was decided that, if followed, it must lead us somewhere ; so we climbed for an hour, silently and stubbornly. It was a most impressive failure. The solitude of the boundless forest about us, and the ghostly effect of the swirling clouds of fog among the tall pines, were awesome. At last a halt was called in a little clearing, the haversacks were opened, and a bit of bread and cheese with a draught of the Jurançon wine was discussed ; while every moment the fog thickened and settled lower. "A little farther!" we said, and with useless persistency we pushed on upward until we heard ahead of us something that sounded like the cry of a child. We halted to listen. It was surely a child's voice. But how came a child up here ? "There are bears in these woods," suggested my mischievous comrade, in a low tone, and we thought of the panther story in Cooper's " Pioneers." Nevertheless, we walked on a bit, and sure enough there were two youngsters playing in front of a woodchopper's hut. We stopped and asked them where was the sawmill of Bious-Artigues ; but they began to whimper with fear at the sight of two strangers coming so suddenly out of the mist. On this the father, a rough looking specimen, stuck his head out of the door, and said something in an incomprehensible jargon. The question being repeated, he answered, in labored French, that the plateau was lower down and that we had come too far. So we turned back, having in all probability

crossed the Spanish frontier after passing to one side
of Bious-Artigues without seeing it. We made good
speed down the corduroy track, but not remembering
exactly the right point at which we should have left
it and turned to the left, we finally found ourselves
completely at a loss as to our route, in the midst of
the thickest and coldest of fogs. After wandering
about a while, and only getting still more confused,
we sat down on a log, in a clearing, and enjoyed the
romantic consciousness of being lost. It was with
more disappointment than relief that I received Hermano's practical suggestion that the first stream we
came to would show us the way down to Gabas.
Probably at that moment the gigantic Pic du Midi was
so near, that, had the atmosphere been entirely clear,
we should have had to throw back our heads and look
upward to see the great fields of snow around its
sharp summit. However, we were destined not to see
it that day. We set forth again, and after twenty
minutes' walking, regained the bank of the Gave de
Bious and followed the stream downward till we
struck the bridle-path. Here we presently met two
young men in blouses, who halted and requested a
light for their cigarettes, perhaps as an excuse for a
little conversation in a *patois* which somewhat resembles that of the Canadian-French, and which shows
the decided influence of the Spanish in several ways,
but principally in the pronunciation of the vowels.

   " You do not fear the fog ? " they said.

" No, but we lost our way. We were looking for
the Plateau of Bious-Artigues."

They asked us what route we had taken, and told us
where we had gone amiss.

" You are foreigners," one of them said. " Are you
English ? "

" No, we are Americans."

" Ah, indeed ! From South America or from North
America ? "

" From the America of the North."

" Ah, that ! I know — that is New York ! "

" Yes, that 's it."

" But you speak English there, is it not so ? "

" Yes, a sort of English."

" And as to politics, how is it in your country ? "

" O, we are all republicans there."

" Good. I would like to go to New York. I have
a cousin who is in your country. In Buenos Ayres."

" Buenos Ayres. But "—

" Is not that city very near your department ? "

" Yes, — yes. It is in New York, in fact. But
there are other parts of the America of the North,
beside. We have other large departments and towns
— several."

" And how large is New York ? "

" Not so large as Paris, but larger than Lyons."

" *Sapristi !* And you have been in Paris ? "

" I believe well ! "

" Ah, there 's a city, eh ? "

" By blue ! "

And so forth. The spokesman had been in Paris, and it was his pride and delight to tell all he knew about it. We talked until his cigarette was smoked up, and then parted company, all hands lifting their hats, and saying, " Au revoir, eh ? " For the Basques append " eh ? " to every sentence.

Bedraggled, chilled, hungry, and in a bad temper, we crawled into the inn at Gabas toward night, and partook of the dubious cheer the establishment had to offer. Then, in the rain and darkness, we pushed on down the valley to Eaux-Chaudes, where we had left our luggage. The next day, looking over our shoulders as we made our way down the hot valley of the Ossau, we saw the Pic du Midi looming up in the bright sunlight and blinking at us in the most provoking manner, as if to say : —

" Yesterday I had on my nightcap, but to-day, if you are of a mind to come back as far as the Plateau of Bious-Artigues, I am ready to show myself — unless I change my mind before you get there."

THE CATALOGUE

OF THE

ART DEPARTMENT

OF THE

NEW ENGLAND EXPOSITION,

⟫1883⟪

Is the most magnificent effort yet made in this country to place
before the public, in a single, compact volume, the results that to this
date have been reached in American Art. It excels all catalogues of
Art that have been produced either in this country or in Europe, and
is designed to serve many other purposes than the one that was the
immediate occasion of its production. It was planned and executed
with immense pains, and absolutely regardless of cost, by John M.
Little, the Chairman, and Frank T. Robinson, the Art Director, of the
Exposition, solely in the interests of the Art and the Art-Industries
of this country. One motive pervades the whole book, and finds
enthusiastic expression in its every page; namely, to produce a
work which for practical value and importance should be attractive
alike to artists, designers, photographers, printers, manufacturers,
indeed to all whose professions and livelihoods are allied with Art
and Art-progress.

It is a large quarto of 300 pages, printed at the Art Age Press of
Arthur B. Turnure, New York, who has succeeded in making it, in
point of paper, printing, and style, an ideal-instance of the typog-
raphy and bibliopegy of the nineteenth century. It contains 63
full-page illustrations, all of which have been judiciously selected
from the most notable works of the best American artists; and, as
produced here, are intended to show the facilities possessed of
artistic illustration and the effectiveness of reproductive methods in
the Art-world.

ORIGINAL ETCHINGS

Of surpassing beauty have been contributed by the following distinguished artists, as well as by others:—

Stephen Parish,	J. C. Nicoll,	C. H. Ritchie,
Thomas Moran,	A. H. Bicknell,	William Hart,
C. A. Platt,	R. C. Miner,	J. A. S. Monks,
Charles Volkmar,		George L. Brown,
B. Lander,		W. F. Lansil.

FULL-PAGE DRAWINGS

Appear by these, among other well-known names:—

Carroll Beckwith,	Carl Chapman,	J. Wagner,
R. Bunner,	R. H. Burleigh,	C. W. Sanderson,
Thomas Robinson,	F. Batchellor,	E. M. Parmenter,
C. D. Hunt,	W. A. Coffin,	Leo Hunter,
Bruce Crane,	F. Childe Hassam,	T. Winthrop Pierce,
E. H. Blashfield,	F. M. Boggs,	Julia Dabney,
R. W. Van Boskerck,	Granville Perkins,	H. M. Knowlton,
R. M. Shurtleff,		Eleanor Matlock.

All persons interested in the historical development, present position, and the prospects of the young American Art School, will find unusually instructive and opportune the series of papers contributed by the ablest living specialists in knowledge of the theories and practice of Art; which considered in their entirety may be said to constitute a literature on Modern Art and Modern Art-tendencies.

The quality and interest of the text is seen from a glance at the

SUBJECTS AND CONTRIBUTORS:

Photography, Edward A. Robinson.
American Art Furniture, A. Curtis Bond.
The Growth of American Art, James Jackson Jarves.
Journalism and Art, M. G. Van Rensselaer.
Portrait Painting, Sidney Dickenson.
Native Painters, Charles DeKay.
American Flower Painters, C. Wheeler.
Etchings, S. R. Koehler.
Landscape Art, William Howe Downes.
Watercolor Painting, Lyman H. Weeks.
American Wood Engraving, Arlo Bates.
Color in Works of Art, R. Riordan.
The Ideal in American Art, Florence Finch.
American Art Journalism, James B. Townsend.
Success in Art, F. T. Lent.
The Art Tariff, L. C. Knight.
Memorial Art, E. H. Silsbee.
What shall American Artists Paint? E. H. Clement.
The Present Conditions of American Art, Arthur B. Turnure.
American Stained Glass, Edward Dewson.
Women as Art Critics, Lillian Whiting.

The book has been produced at the large outlay of $12,000; yet it is offered to the public for the comparatively small sum of $3 a copy. The Publishers invite early and close examination of the volume, confident that it will be found the most considerable contribution yet made to the Art-literature of America, and of inestimable worth to all who are engaged in the furtherance of æsthetic culture, or in the pursuits of Art, whether Design, Painting, Sculpture, Decoration, Photography, Criticism, or in any of the various Art-manufactures and Art-Industries rapidly developing amongst us.

The Publishers reserve to themselves the right of increasing the price after a certain number of copies have been sold.

CUPPLES, UPHAM & CO., Publishers,
283 Washington Street, BOSTON.

. Mailed to any address on receipt of $3.25, postage paid.

Maria Edgeworth,

WITH NOTICES OF HER FATHER AND FRIENDS.

By GRACE A. OLIVER.

Illustrated with portraits and several wood engravings.

Third edition. 8vo. 1 vol. 571 pages, price $2.25. Half calf, $5.00. Tree calf, $7.50.

*** Mailed by publishers, postage paid, on receipt of price.

THIS is a charming record of the literary life, educational and philanthropic efforts, domestic and social history, contacts and friendships of one of the most remarkable women that have ever influenced the world by their pen, or shone in society by their talents. The production of such a work was a debt that society owed to the memory of one so active in its service, and though, perhaps, too long neglected, it is fortunate that at last it has been executed by one so qualified to perform the task by patient research, wide information, and large culture. That this great woman should have found in another woman a biographer so capable and admirable is a very gratifying fact, and well worth the long waiting for; indeed, it almost makes us wish that every supreme instance of high character, literary endeavor and excellence, poetic and imaginative genius, that has appeared or may appear from time to time amongst women, might have the like good fortune to find a Boswell in the growing sisterhood of authors, so able and zealous to do her justice and honor, as the biographer here is to reveal the character and perpetuate the memory of the noble woman about whom she writes. To some extent it must always remain true, that a woman's mind and genius will be best understood and interpreted by a woman, if she happen to be one of real culture and fine discernment; of thoroughly independent habits of mind, and of high literary qualifications. The author of this book has a real genius for biographical writing, but she has not trusted to that genius, when only the labor of hard and wearisome research could avail — she has done immense reading, and gathered her materials from many mines of literary wealth, and from the most diverse sources of information; having done this, her imagination has illumed it all, and her genius has welded it into a consummate biographical unity. Probably no biography of this century has been more conscientiously written, or the facts more carefully gathered together from all known sources, and by all possible means, than in this instance. It seems that the author has crowded into this comparatively small volume a lifetime of study; that she has travelled over, not only the highways of literature during the period covered by the life and efforts of the subject of her biography; but that she knows equally well the by-paths and the shady nooks in which grow the violets, and amidst the fragrance the best thoughts are found. And no endeavor has been wasted, for in accuracy and general interest it must remain amongst the few classics of biographical literature, at once a memorial to the life, genius, and character of MARIA EDGEWORTH, and of the writer's own unique biographical gifts. The subject, too, was well worthy of this great devotion, for in her own particular sphere she is supreme, and deserves a place in the memory of the world beside that of George Sand, Charlotte Bronte, Mrs. Gaskell, and George Eliot, and all the great women who are celebrated for the nobleness of their lives, and the power and beauty of their writings. Her tales and novels have exercised great influence for good on the manners and habits of society, and many of the greatest men have expressed the sense of indebtedness and obligation to her. The chief charms, however, of the book arise not from its showing the intellectual development and literary achievements of a noble woman, but from its revealing her to us, in the real beauty and great refinement of her personality, in society and in intercourse and correspondence with her friends, amongst whom were numbered nearly all the principal persons of the time. This play of heart and imagination in the common relations of life and society, these glimpses and anecdotes of notable persons, this intellectual contact which the book enables us to come into with the poets, novelists, wits, scholars, philosophers, and celebrities of a former generation and age, is one of the richest enjoyments, and one of the greatest benefits conferred by literature. It is not too much to say MARIA EDGEWORTH drew towards her personality the mind and culture of her age, and that from reading this volume we become as familiar with her many friends as with herself; indeed, it is written with such power and realistic touches that she and they become our own familiar companions, and we move in their world. The portraits and illustrations give rare attractiveness to the volume.

Cupples, Upham & Co., Publishers, 283 Washington St., Boston.

Priest and Man; or, Abelard and Heloisa.

AN HISTORICAL ROMANCE.

BY WILLIAM WILBERFORCE NEWTON.

With Fine Illustrations. 1 vol. 12mo. Cloth, elegant, 548 pages. Price, $1.50.

. Mailed by the publishers, postage paid, on receipt of price.

THIS book is a decidedly important addition to the Fiction of America. In its beautiful and accurate presentation of the facts that encircle, in sadness and tragedy, the lives of ABELARD and HELOISA, it is never likely to be surpassed. Amongst the stories of the immortal loves of great men and women, it exercises a spell, the most absorbing, over the imagination, and fascinates to an infinite degree the thoughts and heart of the reader. Truth and accuracy are never sacrificed to the mere glamour of the novelist's art, and yet the mind is carried captive with each successive stage of the story's development, and we almost lose our personality in the personalities of these two deathless lovers. Apart from this book, by the sheer force of their passion and the tragic incidents amidst which their lives were passed, by their culture and the important positions they occupy in the thought-life of their age, by their letters and songs that immortalize their love, both characters were destined to be remembered to the end of time; but the idea was happy in the extreme that led the author into this fruitful field of effort, and to produce so able and masterly a work. The cases are few in which an author, so fortunate in his choice of subject, has, with the aptness and real imaginative genius here displayed, bent his purpose and directed his labor to giving it such noble and artistic expression; the subject is too often marred in the treatment — the characters lose their biographical truthfulness and historic significance in the novelist's use of them for the purposes of his art. Here, however, there are traces on every page of a master's hand, of that clear insight of character and penetration of the secrets of the inner life of mortals, which is the peculiar birthright of genius, and the supreme qualification for success in fiction and all imaginative writing.

The writer has nobly fulfilled the promise of the Preface, in which he says: "This story of a period and this story of a life are based upon the well-known outlines of history. But where the chroniclers are silent, fancy has dictated the fiction of the hour. The passion and tragedy of such a story are not the invention of any writer; they are the strange inheritances of human nature." In short, he has used his art just where he should have done, — used it wisely and judiciously, and so achieved fine results and a large success. He has laid hold and given eloquent utterance to that, in these lives, which makes them of enduring attraction and universal significance in the history of the world. The story of sin and passion, the direful fruits of love in humanity, yet withal, the only ways in which it appears often destined by the will of the gods to reach its redemption and ultimate exaltation and beatification, is a subject that appeals to all, — it appertains to men and women everywhere; it touches each heart and appeals to its sympathies, and thus unites the whole world to those who rejoice, suffer, or endure in it, by the most wonderful of all elective affinities. Thus, though the book transports us into another land and a far century, we nevertheless are rendered quite unconscious of it from the mighty force of its human interest, and the masterly delineation of those passions that make up so large a portion of the life of the world, — not in any one age in particular, but in all ages; and in none more than the present. The love of ABELARD and HELOISA unites their names forever in one joy, sorrow, supreme affection, and undying fame; and it is not too much to say that it enshrines them forever in the memory of the world; unites them as enduringly to humanity as they are united to themselves.

Literary ability, imaginative art, and the creative faculty of genius, have fulfilled their task so well that the book deservedly takes its place amongst the highest works of fiction of this period of our literature ; and may confidently be said to be one, not only of the most entertaining, but instructive of novels, picturing, as it does for us, many of the most notable characters, incidents, circumstances, customs, and institutions of a distant age, in which lived and loved and suffered two of the most fascinating personages in all history. The interest of the book is greatly increased by a fine portrait of HELOISA, and by several beautiful illustrations, in which such prominent facts of the story are represented, as "HELOISA taking the Veil at Argenteuil;" "ABELARD surrounded by his students at the Paraclete;" "A young monk at St. Gildas poisoned by a cup designed for ABELARD;" and, perhaps the most beautiful and pathetic of all, "HELOISA at the Tomb of ABELARD." No book amongst modern novels is calculated to give higher pleasure, or at one and the same time so likely to inform and entertain the mind of the reader.

Cupples, Upham & Co., Publishers, 283 Washington St., Boston.

THE BUSINESS MAN'S ASSISTANT.

1 vol. 12mo. 130 pages. Paper covers, 50 cents; or, bound in **Leatherette**,
Legal Text-book Style, $1.00.

*** Mailed to any address, postage paid, on receipt of price.

THIS little book is offered to the public from the conviction that it will be found of the highest value and convenience in commercial and trade circles. Its author, I. R. BUTTS, has compressed into small compass an immense fund of information on all subjects that concern the business man, whether he be merchant, mechanic, or farmer. Many books have been published bearing this, or a similar title, which have been most inaccurate where they promised to inform, and altogether unreliable in their presentation of the facts and recognized data of the trade-world. This is not the case here; its author is a well-known and highly respected authority, and his " Assistants," designed in the interests of many special professions and handicrafts, enjoy a wide popularity, and are in great request by those for whom they were respectively written. The scheme here is somewhat different from that of his other books, and adopted to make the work of wider service than if it had been shaped solely for the benefit of such as belong to any one particular trade or profession It is found that there are points at which each business touches all other businesses, and each profession involves some acquaintance with every other; the aim, therefore, has been to produce a work that shall, while rendering the utmost aid to each man in his own immediate occupation, still give him that universal information about Industry and Commerce that at any moment he may find himself needing; and without a handbook at his side like this, may be put to great inconvenience, — often large expense. In size it is portable, and suitable for the bag or desk. The following brief outline of some subjects treated will best illustrate its office and worth : —

1. Laws relating to Agent.
2. (a) Forms of Agreement and Contract.
   (b) Laws regulating same.
3. Laws regulating Damages.
4. Forms of Assignment.
5. (a) Forms of Guarantees.
   (b) Laws regulating same.
6. (a) Forms of Awards.
   (b) The Duty of Referees.
7. (a) Forms of Bills of Sale and Bonds.
   (b) Laws regulating Bond.
8. (a) Forms of Deeds.
   (b) Laws regulating same.
9. Forms of Lease.
10. (a) Forms of Mortgages.
    (b) Laws regulating same.
11. Forms of Certificates.
12. (A) Forms of Notice.
    (a) of Intention to Build.
    (b) of Dissolution of Copartnership.
    (c) to Quit, etc.
    (B) Notes, Due Bills, Receipts, Bills of Exchange, Drafts, Orders, Checks.
    (a) Judgment Note, with Laws regulating same.
    (b) Forms of Petitions.
13. Patent Laws.
    (a) Patent Forms.
    (b) New Fees of Patent Office.
    (c) Directions to persons having business with the same.
14. (a) Powers of Attorney.
14. (b) Rules of Law relating to same.
15. Releases, Tenders, Wills.
    (a) Forms of respective Releases.
    (b) Tenders for Work.
    (c) What amounts in various coins are Legal Tenders.
    (d) Forms of Will and Codicil.
16. Practical Rules and Tables.
    (a) Arithmetical, Decimal, Diagrams to find the Square or Superficial Feet in Boards, Marble, Brick Wall, Land, etc.
    (b) To find Area of a Circle.
    (c) To find the Solid Contents in Trees, Timber, Stones, etc.
    (d) To find Capacity in Gallons of Tanks, Reservoirs, etc.
    (e) To find Measures of Weights, Surfaces, Capacity (Dry and Liquid), Length, etc.
    (f) Decimal Approximations for Facilitating Calculations.
17. Lumber Tables.
18. Ready Reckoners.
19. Mechanics' Tables.
20. Interest and Mercantile Tables.
    (a) Of Interest, etc.
    (b) Value of Gold and Silver Coins, and Foreign Currencies.
21. Miscellaneous Tables.
    (a) Rates of Postage, etc.
    (b) Book-keeping, with Directions for Double and Single Entry, etc.

The publishers cordially recommend the book to the business public.

CUPPLES, UPHAM & CO., No. 283 Washington Street., Boston.

AGENTS WANTED EVERYWHERE.

ANNA LÆTITIA BARBAULD.

A MEMOIR,

With many of her Letters, together with a selection from her Poems and Prose Writings.

By GRACE A. OLIVER.

With Portrait. 2 vols. 12mo. Cloth, bevelled, gilt top. Price, $3.00.

THIS is a book of great interest and enduring worth, on one of the most charming characters in English society and English literature during the fifty years covered by the last quarter of the preceding and the first of the present century. Belonging to the Aikin family, many members of which were so singularly accomplished and so devoted to the work of education and progress in days when those who championed these causes were fewer than now, it is gratifying in the extreme to have so accurate and highly appreciative a work as this to put into the hands of those whose enthusiasm and energies are, in these days, devoted to similar ends, — to have so full and beautiful a presentation of one who was herself actuated by the noblest Spirit of Reform, and to catch glimpses, as we do throughout these pages, of many similarly inclined, — especially delightful to be brought into near and intimate contact with the family of benefactors and reformers to which she belonged. Her character and attainments were of so high an order that they deserve to be perpetuated, and will doubtlessly be perpetuated by this book when many of her writings are forgotten; yet there are amongst these selections from her letters, poems, and prose-writings not a few gems that belong to the very choicest things in our literature, than which it were hard to conceive of any more helpful and inspiring to Young England of that or of this day. In her poetry there are lines that bear the impress of the most exalted sentiments and profoundest thought, which made her a peculiar favorite of other poets, especially of Rogers. It was Wordsworth who, on hearing some verses of hers for the first time, said : "It is not often I envy others the honor of their work, but I should like to have written those lines." The author has performed her task with consummate skill and the best of taste, and nowhere is this more evident, or more likely to win praise, than in the many passages throughout the book, where she, with true grace and devotion, stands aside that the one who is her subject may herself be heard, and her wisdom and poetry fall upon our ear as from her own lips.

LIVES OF THE GREAT AND GOOD.

With Portrait. 1 vol. 12mo. Cloth. $1.00.

STORY OF THEODORE PARKER.

By FRANCES E. COOKE.

With an Introduction by GRACE A. OLIVER.

AMONGST the many "lives" of THEODORE PARKER, no one deserves to be wider known than this, and where it is known it must be appreciated. The author, an English lady, has given us in a form more compact than any of the earlier lives, a graphic, realistic, and living picture of THEODORE PARKER as child in the old home, boy on the farm, the earnest student, the patient searcher after truth, the brave heretic, the heroic preacher, and the zealous reformer; and everywhere we see not only the outward, but the inward man, a life ennobled by its love of man and glorified by its love of God, — a character transfigured in that radiant light that "never was on sea or land,"—a spirit resembling the Ideal he followed in the storm and in the calm, in the arduous enterprises with which his life was filled, and in the quiet hour of death. It needs no words to recommend this book to the American public, whose highest pride it must ever be to feel that PARKER was born of them, flesh of their flesh and bone of their bone, and that the forces and influences of his great personality still rest on their institutions and literature, culture and religion; and when universally it is felt, as Lord Coleridge said of him in Boston lately, that here is "one of the highest and greatest souls."

Mailed, postage paid, on receipt of price.

Cupples, Upham & Co., Publishers, 283 Washington St., Boston.

www.ingramcontent.com/pod-product-compliance
Lightning Source LLC
Chambersburg PA
CBHW030607040726
47497CB00008B/2879